As a science teacher at a top secondary school in London, education plays a big part in Emma's life. Having taught in a variety of schools, she was inspired to write this book based on her pupils' different scholastic experiences. Prior to being a teacher, she worked for a global management consulting and professional services firm, in which she was a project management analyst for the retail sector. However, as clichéd as it sounds, she was eager to make a difference to children's lives and dusting off her chemistry degree, she returned to academic life as a teacher and has never looked back.

To all school pupils: past, present and future.

Emma Hollender

SCHOOL 3D

Three sisters. Three schools. Three lives.

AUSTIN MACAULEY PUBLISHERS™

LONDON · CAMBRIDGE · NEW YORK · SHARJAH

A CIP catalogue record for this title is available from the British Library.

ISBN 9781788234689 (Paperback)
ISBN 9781788234696 (Hardback)
ISBN 9781788234702 (E-Book)
www.austinmacauley.com

First Published (2017)
Austin Macauley Publishers Ltd™
25 Canada Square
Canary Wharf
London
E14 5LQ

Contents

1. Fingers Crossed

'R u nervous?'

'No, R u?'

'Lol, no. Ru nervous?'

'U just txtd me tht!'

'Soz typo, wrong persn'

'R u nervous?'

'Yes!!! Rn't u?'

It was late. Three blue lights glowed underneath three duvets on three beds in one room. There was a creak outside on the landing. Instantly, the blue lights dimmed as each phone was buried inside its nearest pillow for safety. Silence. Wait. Count to ten. Parents are asleep, it's all right. Cautiously, the three blue lights flickered into life.

'Y?'

'Y, wat?'

'Y r u scared'

'Coz everthng wl change.'

'What! Ella, you are such a drama queen,' exclaimed Alice.

Ella wished that primary school just continued for ever. It would make things so much easier. The sisters could all stay together. Nothing had to change. However, she knew tomorrow their futures would be decided. Who would go to which secondary school? Would they be separated after all?

As Alice shuffled under the duvet to gaze at her sister in disbelief through the darkness, her phone clunked onto the carpet.

'Shhhhh!' Hazel whispered. 'Use ure fone,' she texted her siblings, reminding them of the dangers of late night communication.

Two creaks on the landing, a light switched on. Someone was in the bathroom. Maybe, but there was another creak, breathing this time. Too close to take the risk. Phones off. Bedtime.

XxxxxxxxxxxX

Six Months Earlier.

Newton Hall School.

The whole world was here.

In the mild September sunshine, the family – Mum, Dad, Alice, Ella and Hazel, stood in a long, snaked queue consisting of many other mums, dads and ten-year-olds, outside a large red brick 1930s school house.

'Excuse me, dear, is there a café nearby for a much-needed coffee?' Mum anxiously asked a tired-looking teacher.

The teacher, policing the obedient queue, smiled sympathetically. 'Well, if you walk across the park, in fifteen minutes, you reach the Woodland Canteen, but I would recommend the tea. Coffee's a bit on the weak side.'

Ella passed a sympathetic glance at her mum; she must be worried. Did a cappuccino calm parents' nerves? Traffic had been terrible. Within a two-mile radius of the school, Dad had given up fighting the stream of cars and parked their battered, silver estate car and walked the remaining distance to school.

The fanfare of horns was like an out-of-tune orchestra. Large four-by-four cars were dropping off kids as if it was a matter of life or death, endangering the lives of everyone else by dramatic overtaking and three-point turns.

'I'll pick up the drinks, dear,' Dad said in a brave voice. 'I'll be back in twenty minutes.'

'Oh, Robin, thanks, darling!' Mum replied as if her problems were already disappearing fast. 'Could you make sure that my coffee is extra hot, too?'

Dad, cautiously crossed the road, just avoiding a car which had decided that driving on the pavement was a faster alternative to the road, and headed across in the direction of the Woodland Canteen.

Mum, waved and then turned to face Alice, Ella and Hazel. 'You are going to be fine, girls. Just enjoy it. Just think about those practice papers and those high marks you got. You'll probably actually find the exam too easy and get bored, but don't forget to check your answers at the end. Please, Hazel, you mustn't day-dream. This is serious—' She paused to look at Ella, whose hands were starting to tremble. 'Well, not that serious, of course, just try your best, that's all.'

Mum broke mid-sentence and looked troubled. Something had distracted her from her long, rambling pep talk.

'Oh, I don't believe it, she's come after all!' she whispered under her breath. 'She promised me that Jodie and Miranda were only applying to Winston College, so why on earth are they here today?'

The triplets turned in the direction of their mum's distracted gaze. They saw two of their fellow classmates at Marlow Primary. Jodie and Miranda were twins. They were also the triplets' cousins and perfect in every way. However, the triplets were not on best friend terms with them.

'Well, my mind's made up,' proclaimed Alice. 'I am going to flunk this Newton Hall test. Year Seven with my terrible two cousins would be a nightmare.'

Hazel giggled and Ella turned pale.

'Oh Mum, they are so smart, we don't stand a chance now,' moaned Hazel. 'They were the first in Year One to know all their times tables. Then in music they made these amazing instruments. Jodie made a cello out of cereal boxes and I just made this empty Pringles jar with dried beans—.'

'Bella!' Mum interrupted Hazel's rant, as the twins' mum, her sister, sauntered up to where they were standing. 'This is a surprise.'

'Katie, darling!' Bella feigned surprise. 'Fancy us meeting like this. What a nice day this is.'

'Yes,' said Mum with as little enthusiasm as she could manage. 'I thought Jodie and Miranda were going to only apply to Winston's College.'

'Well, yes,' Bella's lips twisted into a wistful smile. 'But I thought it would be excellent practice for them both to try this one, just for fun. They love exams, you see. So dedicated, my girlies.'

Mum's eyes narrowed, hearing one of Bella's favourite phrases, "Just for fun". "Just for fun" was the reason why Jodie and Miranda had daily tutoring in every subject, since they were able to walk. "It's just like tennis practice," Bella used to say at the monthly school coffee mornings. "It's just exercise for the brain, super healthy!"

In her ever more nervous state, Ella's hands trembled so much that she dropped her pink pencil case on the pavement. Alice decided that picking it up with her hands would be too easy. Instead, she sandwiched it between her shoes and did a small jump. It flew through the air and somehow managed to bounce off Jodie's head, squashing the ears of her Minnie Mouse headband.

'Ouch, that seriously hurt, Alice.' Jodie glared at Cousin Alice.

'Ha-ha, if you can't even hold a pencil case, Ella, how do you expect to use it in an exam?' Miranda smirked.

'Alice!' Mum said, trying her best to sound angry. 'Do be careful not to injure your poor cousin.'

'Come on, darlings,' Bella turned to the terrible twins. 'We are in the first sitting, don't want to miss our fun now, do we?'

As the three sauntered away, the friendly-faced teacher, who had also been a coffee adviser, waved at the triplets. 'All right, you three, time to come with me and leave Mum. You'll see her in just over an hour's time. Say 'bye for now.'

Alice gave Mum a hug, Hazel gave her a friendly high five and Ella gave a watery smile.

'Good luck, Triple Trouble,' said Mum using the parents favourite nick name for the triplets, 'love you!'

Mum waved and then turned to see Dad return, perfectly timed, from his park trip with the much-anticipated hot drinks.

Mum accepted the hot coffee gratefully. Unfortunately for Dad, Bella assumed that the second coffee was for her and took it with a large, crocodile-style grin. The three parents sat on the bench outside the school and waited for an hour. They were in such deep thought about their daughters, they sat in near-silence, Dad feeling distinctly coffee deprived but too scared of Mum's sister Bella to say as much.

Katie Platt was drinking her coffee thoughtfully. Newton Hall was the best grammar school in London.

Dad joked that succeeding in the entry exam was harder than winning the lottery. Had Katie done the right thing, submitting them all for the exam? It would be amazing if they all were accepted, but would they be? Hazel found lessons easy but also loved learning as much as possible. The other two of her daughters were trickier. Both clever, yes, but they concentrated their talents on other things. Ella adored music and devoted all her time to practising the violin and Alice's dream was to be an Olympic athlete.

And now Bella was also here with her girls. The cousins' relationship wasn't the friendliest. To be honest, though, Katie reflected, it was probably due to the fact that everything they had ever done in their lives was a competition. The triplets were the same age as their twin cousins and at the same school and everything they did/had ever done was compared. It was this that had created a fence of rivalry.

XxxxxxxxxxxX

Oak Academy

The playground was huge.

The pupils at Oak Academy, also called 'Wasps', due to their yellow and black uniform, laughed as they played a hybrid sport of football and basketball. At the far end of the playground was a large boat-shaped building housing a twenty-five metre pool. Alice loved it. Did they have lessons at all, or was it just sport? This place was amazing.

Ella gazed uncertainly around. There must have been over two thousand students here. Why did the school need high concrete walls? Who were the bigger kids in the corner, who looked distinctly unfriendly? Why the signs everywhere reminding kids that, "Doing the nice thing is the right thing!"

Hazel was bored; she could have been actually putting her time to good use. She could have been swotting up for her latest science test or tackling some of her special Mensa puzzles. Instead, it was another day and another school.

There was a scraping of chairs as lots of Year Six students and their keen mums and dads took their seats. A younger woman, no more than forty years old, beamed at her audience.

'Welcome, one and all, to Oak Academy. This is a school where you grow in academic ambition and become a model citizen of the future.' She paused, surveying her crowd. Hazel stifled a yawn.

A baby started crying and the embarrassed mum rushed her out. A keen parent put up their hand and asked about the choice of subjects at GCSE.

The head happily seized on the opportunity to show off the number of subjects they offered. Alice looked horror-struck and yelled out, 'What! You mean, you actually teach here? I thought we could just do sport all day.'

Mum flushed pink. 'Alice,' she hissed, 'do think before shouting out like that, remember your manners!'

Surprisingly, the head grinned and appeared flattered. 'Well, Alice, here at Oak Academy, we have a sports specialism. This means our sports facilities are outstanding.' She paused to a satisfied parental sigh of approval. 'Unfortunately for you, though, we are a school too, but lessons aren't too bad, I promise!'

XxxxxxxxxxxX

Winston College

The floor was an ice rink.

Perfectly polished, the shiny tiles acted as both an excellent mirror and a skaters' paradise. Ella stroked her violin and waited to be summoned to a far room, where music was floating out. Well, "floating out" was a little exaggeration; "stumbling out" would be more apt, as the player was clearly a little hesitant about the piece.

Around a large mahogany table were large squashy sofas, on which similarly anxious ten-year-olds sat, hugging their musical instruments. A large pink plate sat in the centre of the table, crammed full of every type of biscuit imaginable. Normally, Ella would have devoured them but at that moment she felt a little nauseous with nerves. Astrid, a confident girl with blond hair and patent shoes was steadily munching her way through them and in her boredom, had devised a league table of which had the best crunch.

'Well, my mum's aunt actually knows the head, you see. So, based on family connections, I am bound to get into Winston's,' proclaimed Clara, a small girl with dark hair and glasses. 'Nowadays, it's all about networking, that's what my mum says and she *knows*.'

Astrid paused thoughtfully during a jammy dodger, as if about to add to the discussion, but thought better of it and resumed her battle of the biscuits by squashing the custard cream and ginger nut together to form a type of biscuit double decker.

Ella wished that Alice and Hazel were with her. Alice had no patience with girls like Clara and Hazel was always funny in her moans. The result of all three in the room would have been entertaining.

'Ella Platt.' A tall, willowy man, about the age of Ella's dad, appeared by the music room door. He smiled at Ella. 'We're ready for you now.'

Ella took a deep breath and walked towards the door. A young girl brushed past her, leaving the room and Ella grimly noticed it was one of her Terrible Two cousins.

Jodie shuffled out of the room and glared darkly. 'Mummy told me that she doesn't think that you have had enough music lessons to get in here,' she said encouragingly.

'Um, I think you may have forgotten something, Ella,' Clara called after her helpfully.

Ella whirled around to see Clara looking a little pompous, having announced this coded message. Astrid cheerily waved a chocolate bourbon in the direction of her abandoned violin, which was waiting patiently for its owner to remember it on the sofa.

'Oh,' Ella looked mortified. 'Oops. I guess I might need that.' Then she turned to Jodie and smiled, pretending it had been a deliberate tactical manoeuvre. 'You see, even though I am good, even a maestro can't play without their instrument.'

2. Growing Apart

'Happy B-day 2 u'

'Happy B-day 2 u'

'Happy B-day dear us!'

'☺ ☺ ☺'

The triplets chortled under the bedclothes and signed off their text messages with different animal smiley face emojis. The old-fashioned birthday song was clearly made especially for them. Alice threw her duvet on the floor and jumped on Ella's bed. Hazel reached for her fluffy dressing gown and flopped over in her slippers to join them.

'Ouch,' laughed Ella. 'That was my little toe you just bounced on.'

'Better?' laughed Alice, as she bounced on the other one in an attempt to balance the pain.

'Guys, let's wake up the parents. I need presents on my birthday and I have had to wait an entire year!' Hazel tugged at Ella's duvet and caused Alice to land on the floor with a bump.

'Do you think the post will have arrived?' asked Ella hesitantly.

'Do you really care if Auntie Bella has sent you a soppy flower card?' replied Alice.

'Well, what grateful nieces she has. Lucky Auntie Bella!' exclaimed Dad, who had magically appeared in their bedroom.

'Ha-ha, only joking, Dad,' said Alice. 'I just wish she would actually give us something useful, like a voucher or cash. Anyway, eavesdropping on your daughters' conversation is rude.'

'Hmmm, charming young lady, you are,' chuckled Dad. 'Come on then, Triple Trouble, downstairs we go.'

Alice bounced out of the room first. Ella paused to dig her dressing gown from under the bed. 'I didn't mean *birthday post*,' she whispered darkly to Hazel. 'I meant the *school post*.'

'Oh,' replied Hazel. In all the morning excitement, she had completely forgotten that the first of March wasn't just their birthday but also eleven-plus results day. 'I dunno, I guess so.' She paused at the top of the stairs meaningfully, and put her hand on Ella's fluffy arm. 'Don't tell Alice, though, I think she has forgotten for the time being.'

XxxxxxxxxxxX

The kitchen was colourful.

Streamers of pink, purple and green, to satisfy each of the triplets' favourite colours, covered the ceiling.

The table was coated in sparkly confetti and the correct favourite colour balloon saying, 'Eleven Today' was tied to each chair.

'Happy Birthday times three, darlings,' sang Mum.

'Oh, Mum, the kitchen looks really cool,' purred Ella.

'Look at the cake,' said Alice, as she pointed to a round chocolate fudge gateau in the middle of the cereal boxes. It was decorated with a large white chocolate iPhone, which said "Hpy Bday" on the screen.

'Aw, you really tried hard,' said Hazel, smiling at Mum in as patronising a way as possible. 'Next time, I will give you some texting lessons first, though.'

'Is anything missing?' asked Alice wistfully.

'Like what?' asked Dad with a twinkle in his eye.

'Ummm, like presents?' asked Alice cautiously.

'Well, seeing as now you are all so old—' began Dad, teasing.

'Open your cards to find out,' smiled Mum, rolling her eyes.

Alice ripped off the top of the envelope without a second's wait. Hazel was a close second and Ella was the reliable third.

'Whoop, whoop!' rejoiced Alice. 'Finally, we can choose!'

All three triplets held gift vouchers in their hands for their favourite department store.

'We thought we would go first thing after breakfast,' said Dad. 'I can't stand Oxford Street on the best of days, but if we get there early enough, we should miss the worst of the crowds.

'Then we are going to your favourite place for lunch, Nando's, before your afternoon birthday treat!'

'Yay, Mum!' said Ella. 'I thought we were too old for birthday treats now. Where are we going?'

'It's a musical, based on the Wizard of Oz—' began Dad.

'OMG!' gasped Alice. 'The troublesome twins saw it for their birthday and have been boasting about it ever since. Super, we can boast on Monday and there are three of us, so we will win boasting!'

Just then the phone rang. It always did on their birthdays at about this time. The triplets sighed; they were just about to tuck into their annual birthday breakfast of Coco Pops and Frosties with a slice of the birthday cake. They hated their breakfast being disturbed and they knew it was Auntie Bella.

Mum searched for the phone, which, amazingly, had been in the oven (luckily not turned on) and answered. 'Hello, Bella,' she said cheerfully. 'Yes, the triplets are just tucking into their birthday breakfast. Then we are going into town to do some special pressie shopping before seeing the new musical I was telling you about.'

Auntie Bella said something quietly and Mum paused, looking slightly worried. 'Um, no, the post hasn't arrived yet. However, Triple Trouble can't wait to get your card.'

She paused again. 'I don't know yet, I will tell you later. Got to go now, busy day ahead. Byeee!'

'We love you, Auntie Bella,' chorused the triplets, now eagerly eyeing up the birthday cake for a special birthday slice.

Half an hour later, the triplets were engaged in the usual dressing-up race for the outside. It was a cold March. Nine gloves, three scarves, three hats, three coats and a pile of mismatched shoes were happily being un-muddled by Ella.

As they were just about to go, Dad called them back. 'Oh, the musical this afternoon doesn't allow mobile phones. You'll have to leave them here for now.' Hazel eyed her phone longingly. 'Please, Dad. A whole day without it—'

'Phone or birthday treat?' asked Dad uncompromisingly.

Hazel glowered and dug her phone out of her glove, placing it on the table with Alice's and Ella's.

Alice was already skipping down the street towards the bus stop. Hazel linked arms with Ella. 'Totally unfair move by Dad,' she said.

Ella grinned uneasily. 'Yes, but you know why.'

Hazel said, 'What? Why we are not allowed phones and are leaving rather early for shopping?'

Ella sighed. 'Remember, our results come out today. They don't want us to know in case—'

'In case what?' Alice had reversed her skipping and was now listening in.

Ella changed subject rapidly. 'Race you to the bus stop. One, two, three, go!'

XxxxxxxxxxxX

Home, five p.m.

Shopping was heavy.

As they affectionately took their new gifts upstairs, the triplets agreed it had been a great birthday, 'One of the best!' They were cautious never to say, "The best", as they wisely considered it was not a fair comparison, since they could not clearly remember the first three parties in their early lives.

'Girls, come downstairs. Teatime, the kettle's boiling,' Dad yelled.

Alice made a face as she hated the taste of tea, but was comforted by the thought of another birthday cake slice.

Arm in arm the triplets bounded downstairs and took their places at the table. Mum and Dad had a mug of tea in hand already. Mum had given up wondering if the triplets would ever like tea, and instead they each had a large mug of fizzy orange juice with a generous slice of birthday cake. Mum looked a little anxious and set down her mug of tea next to three letters on the table.

'Oh, more birthday cards,' sighed Alice gleefully. 'So much fan mail, when you are as popular as us.'

However, the letters were too formal to be birthday wishes. They were stamped with an official crest and addressed to Mr and Mrs Platt, the triplets' parents.

'Oh, hang on, is that what I think it is?' asked Hazel worriedly. 'The results day letters?'

Sure enough, as the triplets stared in alarm at the letters, there was no mistaking the familiar school crests, which would contain the news of their new school. Ella decided the best bet was to hide under the table. Hazel had buried her face in her hands and was emitting a loud wail and Alice just sat at the table, punching her "Eleven Today" balloon.

'Err, as there are three letters,' said Dad cautiously, 'we thought that you could open one each.' It was clear the parents were out of their comfort zone, thought Hazel. She guessed this would only happen once in their whole school life.

Alice pounced on the first envelope from Oak Academy. Ella took a large intake of breath.

'Dear Mr and Mrs Platt,' she read, trying to sound suitably senior. 'As you know, your three daughters were registered for eleven-plus entry to Oak Academy. We are pleased to inform you that each of your daughters, Alice, Ella and Hazel, has been awarded a place at our school—' she paused.

'Well done, us!' Alice jumped up. 'I am definitely going. Did you see the amazing sports facilities they have? Decision made! Mum, when can we buy the uniform?'

Mum laughed, then pointed to the remaining two letters on the table. 'Ella, darling, you can choose the next envelope if you like.'

'Humph!' moaned Hazel. 'What about me?'

'Now, now, Hazel, we are going in alphabetical order, it's only fair,' said Dad in an annoyingly patronising tone.

'Huh,' replied Hazel, distinctly nonplussed. 'Fair if your name isn't at the end of the alphabet!'

Ella emerged from under the table. She was pale and her fingers trembled as she reached out for the second envelope, which carried a silver crest for Winton's College.

'Dear Mr and Mrs Platt,' she began.

'So far, so good,' interrupted Alice.

'Shhh,' whispered Hazel impatiently.

Ella resumed, 'I am pleased to inform you that Ella has been awarded a musical scholarship at Winton's College. I would be grateful if you could confirm acceptance of her place at the school by—'

Ella had frozen in a happy trance. Mum, Dad, Alice and Hazel gave her a big bear-like hug.

'Well done, darling!' said Mum. 'We are so proud.'

'Yeah, us too,' said Hazel, giving her sister a friendly pinch. 'I knew that the musical maestro could do it.'

Hazel then absent-mindedly picked up the final letter left on the table. It bore the dark crimson crest of

Newton Hall. She opened it and read it quietly, then looked around.

'Well?' asked Alice tentatively. 'What did it say?'

'Umm—well, I got in,' replied Hazel quietly.

The others were silent and Alice, having digested it quicker than the others, then replied with, 'Just you?'

'Yes,' replied Hazel in a mouse-like voice. She didn't make eye contact with Ella or Alice, but just looked at Mum and Dad in a strange sort of way.

'Well done, Hazel! That's amazing!' Ella was the first to break the silence.

Alice gave her sister a friendly slap on the back, but less enthusiastically than usual.

'Group hug, team.' said Dad. 'All for one and one for all!'

Just then the phone rang and the triplets left the table quickly for fear of having to speak with one of their annoying relatives. Alice went upstairs to get changed for swimming practice. Ella went to grab her violin for her lesson and Hazel curled up with a book on the sofa. Mum was still on the phone and so Dad drove Alice to the local pool and Ella walked up the hill to her music lesson.

XxxxxxxxxxxX

Bugging phones was tricky.

Hazel reluctantly put down her book, suspended on a cliffhanger chapter and decided to be a spy on behalf of her sisters. She crawled quietly into the upstairs bedroom, nestled between the armchair and double bed and picked up the other phone handset. Holding it upside down and muffling her breathing in her thick wool hoody, she tuned in to Mum and Auntie Bella's chatter. First, Mum recalled the delights of the musical to Auntie Bella, who of course had already seen it with Miranda and Jodie. It seemed to Hazel, as she naughtily listened in, that both her mum and her aunt were determined to prove that their production of the musical was the best. Auntie Bella had taken Jodie and Miranda to see a new play based on one of the children's favourite books, as according to her, "Musicals were very last year".

Then her tone changed as she described the eleven-plus school results that afternoon.

'Well, I don't know, yet,' replied Mum. 'They haven't actually decided which schools they will choose. Well, okay, Alice only has one choice. Still, Oak Academy will suit her. I think for all three, though, it needs some time to sink in. Gosh, what a nightmare if all three went to different schools.'

'Mmm,' pondered Auntie Bella. 'Yes, you would have to hope that parents' evenings were on different days. Oh, and imagine their twelfth birthday party, you would have three different classes to invite.'

'Yes,' replied Mum, sounding distinctly unenthusiastic. Birthday parties were the last thing on her mind at the moment. 'But honestly, would it work?'

'It worked for us, didn't it?' Auntie Bella reminded her.

'Oh, well, I suppose.' Mum paused for thought. She had forgotten about their own schooldays. However, of course, she and Bella had indeed gone to different secondary schools.

Hazel pressed the receiver closer to her ear, this was news! She had assumed, logically so, that her mum and aunt as sisters had gone to the same school. She took out her new sparkly purple diary, one of her birthday gifts. Just as she was an avid reader, she was also a budding fiction writer. In the "notes" section, she wrote with a flourish, using her new metallic indigo fountain pen, under the title, *Questions for Mum*, "Where did you go to secondary school?"

'Anyway, Bella—' Mum stopped. 'Gosh, bad reception on your line today? Is your connection all right?'

'Perfectly fine here, Katie. Must be something on your end. Anyway, got to dash, Bonio wants his walk and the pup won't wait for his toilet break for long. I shall call you back in a few minutes.'

At this point, Hazel carefully replaced the receiver and crawled back into her bedroom, where her book awaited on her purple bean bag.

Within a minute of becoming re-immersed in her adventure spy novel, Hazel was disturbed by Mum.

'Are you all right, Hazel, darling?' Mum appeared at the doorway. 'The three of you girls seemed a little quiet after all today's excitement.'

'Yeah, Mum. Thanks for an amazing day. I guess we were all just a bit tired from all the activity and news.' Hazel carefully squashed her book flat on its spine on the floor.

'Oh, Hazel, do be careful with the new book. What has it done to deserve being squashed by you?'

'It's practical, Mum. I can find my place easily and without a book mark.'

'Hmmm—' sighed Mum. However, as Hazel stared at her, she noticed that she had an ulterior motive. Sure enough, Mum knelt down by the beanbag and then picked up the book. 'Hazel, we are really proud of you. I mean, the competition to get into Newton Hall was huge and you must have done brilliantly in the exam.'

Hazel flushed. This was embarrassing, but she had to admit it was nice of Mum to tell her of her pride. It was true, she had worked hard, super hard. She had done all the practice paper packs they had been given at school. She had even stolen a couple of spare question packs from her cousin Jodie. Well, the terrible two never bothered to actually do the work set by their tutor, the poor questions obviously needed to be given a home by Hazel.

'Um, Mum?' began Hazel, stroking her purple sparkly diary. 'When you went to secondary school—'

Just then the phone rang again. Mum jumped up, 'Be back soon, Hazel.'

Hazel heard Mum jogging into the upstairs bedroom to pick up the receiver.

Hazel heard Mum in a weary tone say, 'Oh, hello, Bella, again!'

Hazel put down her book, carefully squashing its spine once more on the page she was reading and crept to listen in to the mum of the terrible two, Jodie and Miranda. Now Bella was going to reveal the fate of her cousins in the eleven-plus exams. Of course, it wasn't just them receiving their results today, it was everyone.

Feigning a desire to have another drink, Hazel slipped downstairs into the kitchen where the other phone receiver was waiting patiently for the triplet spy.

XxxxxxxxxxxX

Ella

Ella wanted to yell with happiness.

As she walked up the hill to her music lesson, she was skipping every other step. She had done it! She had got into the most prestigious school nearby for music. Already, she loved Winston's so much. Too much? She remembered the shiny marble, patchwork floors, the oak panelling, the kindly music master. She even recalled her interview pals, Astrid and for some rose-tinted reason, the rather pompous Clara. Would they have also been offered a place? Oh please, let Astrid be offered a place, she thought, Alice and Hazel would be bound to like her.

But then, what about Alice and Hazel? Where would they decide to go? Well, for Alice, at least, that choice was easy, she would have to choose Oak Academy. Ella shuddered, it had all just seemed too big and loud there. Would Hazel choose Newton Hall or Oak Academy? Like Ella, Hazel wasn't naturally sporty and so had not been so overwhelmed by the impressive swimming pool and sports pitches at the academy. Ella had seen her researching the Newton Hall uniform the other day on her phone; navy jumper and skirt with a pink shirt and gold tie. Apparently, they called Newton Hall pupils 'Butterflies' due to their rather colourful uniform ensemble.

She reached the red door of the old cobbled street, where her music teacher lived.

'Oh, I do like your pink music case, Ella!' Miss Wood smiled down at the beaming mousy-haired triplet. She had noticed, of course; she had good taste.

The leather music case had been the birthday gift that Ella had awarded herself that very morning. It was decorated with silver music notes and pinned by a treble clef clip.

'It's my birthday, I mean our birthdays, today!' gleefully chirped Ella.

'Lucky me,' said Miss Wood. 'I always find that students play music best on their birthdays.'

Ella kicked off her boots on the door mat – Miss Wood was most particular about no shoes in her house – and walked up the wonky staircase of the old house. The houses along her street were all of the same old construction. To a newcomer, they would have felt rather dizzy inside as the stairs sloped as you ascended them and the floors of the rooms sloped in the opposite direction.

As Ella placed her violin case on the floor, Barley, Miss Wood's toffee-coloured Labrador, appeared behind the sofa. He rubbed his wet, cold nose in Ella's hair.

'So, Ella dear,' Miss Wood asked curiously, 'what's your exciting school news?'

Ella looked up, patted Barley on the head and gave a beaming grin. 'Winston's said yes! I got a scholarship, Miss Wood, err, maybe thanks to you. Oops, sorry. Would you like a present for being such a good music teacher?'

Now it was Miss Wood's turn to grin happily. 'Ha-ha, your happiness is the best present I could wish for, my dear! Oh, you will have a good time. You can join Junior Orchestra in your first term, I will put in a good word for you. Then, in your second term, you should audition for Violetas, exclusively for violins, normally just for the more senior girls, but they will make an exception for you as they did for me.' Miss Wood sat down on the sofa, giving Barley an affectionate squeeze of the ears, which he seemed a little puzzled about.

Ella, who was slowly preparing her bow, having caked it in rather too much rosin, stopped. 'Hang on. You mean, Miss Wood, did you go there too?'

'Indeed, I was an old "Wintonian". Best days of my life, Ella. You will love it there.' She stopped for a moment, clearly reminiscing happily before resuming, 'Even though I went in the dark ages, you understand.

No looking at old school photos for evidence of a young Miss Wood, now, Ella.'

Ella laughed. Miss Wood was not as old as the dinosaurs, as she frequently suggested she was. Maybe some of the older teachers had even taught her. Oh, thought Ella, hugging her violin, Winston's was certainly going to be fun.

XxxxxxxxxxxX

Alice

Alice dived into the pool.

She wore her new goggles and swimsuit, bought only that morning as her birthday present. Gosh, already the birthday celebrations seemed ages ago. Was it really still the same day? She moved quickly through the water, barely causing a ripple on the surface of the pool. Her goggles were good, no water seeped into the lens and yet her eyes were wet.

Stupid Alice, she thought. The only sister to only have one choice of school. Hazel and Alice would both choose their other nice schools. Was Alice's school nice? Hang on, but it was nice, she reflected deeply. She had loved its sports facilities, its large playground, its lively community feeling. So why was she sad?

Dad was watching her on the seating above the gala pool with a couple of other parent spectators. He didn't normally stay to watch her. She was in a squad. She was so good that she competed in the squad two years above her expected age group. It was by accident that she had discovered her swimming talent.

She had only been three years old, when in a fit of annoyance waiting for Mum to blow up her arm bands on holiday, she had just jumped into the deep end. Mum shrieked at Dad to dive in, but Dad had already seen the impressive Alice in action. She just calmly swam in elegant breast stroke to the safety of the shallow end. Hazel clapped and said, 'Me, Me!' Mum had laughed weakly and denied any more of her children trying the stunt and decided they should all go for lunch in a café away from the poolside for a while. Luckily for Mum, it was only Alice who persisted. The other two were more interested in going down the various slides than doing laps of the pool when barely out of their toddler years.

Fortunately, as Alice got changed, the other girls did not ask about the eleven-plus results. They had forgotten that she was at least two years their junior. They admired her for her advanced swimming prowess; she was the best breast stroke and fly competitor of the two hundred metre race. Some of the girls were discussing how their little sisters had received their results today, but Alice speedily towel dried her hair and decided to leave instead of waiting in the long queue for the hair dryers.

Dad was waiting, smiling, standing by the snack vending machine.

'Final birthday treat,' he said. 'Any edible treat you like!'

Alice thought deeply as she stared at the glass vending machine displaying a metallic rainbow of wrappers housing each snack.

She punched in the number seventy-one and out came a particular favourite of the triplets, a chocolate bar, "Packed with goodness", as she liked to say. Caramel, nuts, white and milk chocolate with a biscuit centre. Pure bliss.

Then she paused. 'But can I get two, Dad?' she asked longingly. 'I want to give one to Ella and one to Hazel as a "well done" card.'

Dad stopped, bent down and looked into her eyes. 'Well, in that case we need three. One for each of you. You all deserve a "well done" card as you say.'

'Not me,' said Alice, in an unusually quiet Alice voice.

'Yes, you. You are going to love Oak Academy, Alice. They are delighted to have you! They called me up when you were swimming just now, to personally invite you for advanced trials for their swim and tennis squads.'

A warm glow burst into Alice's still slightly wet swimming-hair head. 'Really? You are positive? They asked for me, specially?'

'Yep,' replied Dad, proudly smiling. 'They said you were the first call on their list, even above the county players. Apparently, you made quite an impact with the Sports Department, when you expressed surprise that this school actually had lessons and not just sport. They said, you showed the right level or commitment. He paused again.

Alice was now happily eating her well-deserved swim/school treat.

'So what do you say, Alice?' he asked. 'Do we give Oak Academy a thumbs up?'

3. First Day

'R u asplp?'

'Not now!'

'LOL!'

'Go 2 slp!'

'☺, 1st Day!'

'Go Oak Academy;

'Go WINSTONS!'

'Go 2 slp u 2!'

Hazel was not a fan of early morning wake-up calls. Over the last year, one of her favourite pastimes of reading after midnight, "As the adventure became more exciting in the dark," often made her slower to start in the morning compared to her more active sisters.

Their phones buzzed in a ringtone clashing morning alarm. Alice had the *Sports Today* theme tune, Ella had chosen a well-known classical theme, and Hazel had her favourite boy band pop song to wake her up slowly. Their uniforms were waiting on their green, pink and purple bean bags. They had waited a long time for this day.

'Smile!' said Dad.

He was waiting at the bottom of the staircase with his camera poised. Alice, Ella and Hazel linked arms in true triplet style and waltzed dangerously down the stairs. It was getting increasingly harder to do as they had all grown a little over the long summer holidays.

'Say cheese!' He focused the lens on Triple Trouble.

'Cheddar, Dairylea, mouse cheese!' They chorused their favourite cheeses as they jumped the final step.

As they sat tucking into their breakfast, fighting over the cereal packets. Mum smiled over her morning coffee. They looked very colourful as well as cheerful.

Alice wore a black blazer and tunic with a yellow shirt. Oak Academy pupils were also called 'Wasps' and Alice was very happy about this, as it was also the name of a well-known sports team. Ella, on the other hand, wore a maroon polo shirt and jumper. She could wear whatever else she liked and had settled for a new pair of grey jeans with gleaming white converse. Finally, Hazel wore a bright uniform of pink shirt, navy jumper, skirt and the unmistakably golden tie. Newton Hall pupils were called 'Butterflies' for a reason.

Dad was busy checking work emails on his phone whilst simultaneously drinking coffee and hunting out the marmalade for his toast. Hazel looked up from solving the crossword on the back of her Space Crispies cereal packet and shook her head. Their parents enforced a strict ban about the triplets' mobile phone usage at the table, but seemingly forgot that it would only be fair if they lived by the same rules.

Mum was squashing three different coloured (green, pink and purple) containers into their already full-to-bursting rucksacks. Alice was trying to see through the plastic cover to see if the lunch was sufficiently cool. Hopefully it contained a sports snack bar, the oaty/chocolate one.

Ella was tapping a melody using her teaspoon, half-filled orange juice glass and cereal bowl. At the grand finale of the piece, she gave a resounding tap on Hazel's filled mug, which inexplicably shattered. There was a sudden tsunami of hot chocolate which swamped the table.

Dad swiped his phone off the table and jumped up to grab the kitchen paper to control the flood.

Just then the doorbell rang. 'Hazel, that's your bus. Go, go, darling.' Mum said. She quickly looked Hazel up and down to make sure that no chocolate had stained her new uniform. Ella, guilty with her musical mistake, gave her an apologetic hug and wished her luck.

Alice, meanwhile, was checking that Mum had packed the right swimsuit for her swim trials after school.

'Go, Triple Trouble, before you cause any more destruction.' Dad waved.

'Just have fun, girls,' called Mum anxiously at the threshold.

All three triplets, rucksacks on backs, joined hands for the last time.

'Good luck!' they whispered to each other as they parted ways. Ella walked down the hill clutching her music case, Alice jogged upwards towards Oak Academy and Hazel, happy in the prospect of not having to walk at all, boarded her new school bus to Newton Hall.

XxxxxxxxxxxX

Winston's College

The cat watched with interest.

About twenty-five new pupils, dressed in their brand new maroon polo shirts, climbed the stairs of the old schoolhouse. For some reason, the first year classroom was situated on the attic floor. Perhaps the logic was that as they were smaller in size than the other years, they would be the quietest occupants above the other classrooms. However, what the young students lacked in size they made up for in energy and they raced upwards to their new room in a loud stampede.

Ella looked around at her new class. Were there any familiar faces? She expected to see at least two, Jodie and Miranda. Sure enough, Jodie was bagging a popular desk by the window even though another rather large girl was already sitting on the chair. What a shame Winston's had accepted her too. The girl seemed not to care about this desk security threat and just sat, nonchalantly staring at the playground far below. The playground was good by secondary school standards. The headmaster understood that even older pupils liked to play games and there was a magnificent climbing frame and five swings waiting patiently for break time.

The large girl turned around as the black cat leapt onto the desk and to Ella's delight, she realised the girl was Astrid, the friendly biscuit-eating girl at her music audition. Ella decided to take the neighbouring desk and gave Astrid a friendly punch as she sat down. Fortunately for Jodie, she had spotted a new associate in crime, Clara, and retreated to the desks at the back of the classroom by the bookcase. Jodie and Clara had met on interview day and realised a mutual sharing in beliefs; only speaking to people they deemed important. They would certainly be firm friends.

Astrid grinned at Ella. 'Hello again! I was keeping my fingers and toes crossed you would get in. It clearly worked because here you are.'

'Well done you, too,' Ella laughed. Then she took a dark look at the back of the classroom. 'Shame about those two, though.'

Astrid turned and saw Jodie and Clara exchanging phone numbers in their brand new iPhones. 'Yep, well, there are always going to be annoying people in the world,' reflected Astrid deeply,' 'Although she didn't get a scholarship,' Astrid whispered, pointing at Jodie. 'Rumour has it that she was the worst violinist that has ever auditioned for the musical award. Her sister didn't make it, though, their mum had to plead just to get Jodie a place.'

At that illuminating moment, a young woman with blond frizzy hair appeared at the door way. The black cat, Carbonel, decided to abandon his current occupation of the teacher's desk and curled up by the empty fireplace. Miss Walker was their class teacher. In the first year they would have all their lessons, except science and sport, in their classroom and Miss Walker would teach them. She had clear blue eyes, perhaps made extra blue by contact lens and an efficient manner.

The first activity was to hand out timetables. Half the class at once gleefully reached for their pencil cases and began to colour code their lessons, using their sparkling new pencil case stationery. Ella glanced down the schedule for the day: Latin first and then music followed. At lunchtime, she was to attend the orchestra auditions. Astrid played the trumpet and would be trying out. Ella hastened a look to where Jodie was sitting to see if she had brought her violin too. Thankfully, it looked like she had given up the battle and instead was going to expand her charming social circle by befriending Clara.

Latin proved surprisingly active. They were learning the first three tenses of Latin verbs. After ten minutes, Miss Walker stopped the class to quiz them. If they failed on the present tense, they had to do star jumps. If they failed on the future tense it was sit-ups and if they failed on the imperfect tense, they had to do press-ups. Ella thought the patterns of verbs were quite musical and took to them easily. Astrid was less fortunate and at the end of the lesson tumbled into her chair exhausted, after several rounds of star jumps and press-ups.

'Phew, I'm exhausted,' she said. 'I hope they give us decent biscuits at break.'

XxxxxxxxxxxX

Newton Hall

Team Building was messy.

Each group had spaghetti and marshmallows. Their mission was to build the tallest tower. Hazel's group were doing well; she noticed with some pride that they were listening to her. Through her extensive reading, she had read about famous building construction before and decided that the Eiffel Tower model was the best choice. Their masterpiece, though swaying slightly, had reached an impressive height of nearly one metre. They had ten minutes left.

The class of 7N were in the playground. Clearly, the teacher had thought wisely that the tower challenge had great potential for mess and thus the outside was better than making a classroom rather sticky. In her group were Hazel's new two best friends, Patrick and Ayushi. Ayushi was a super brain at maths. She was carefully calculating the exact height that their edible tower could achieve before breaking point. She had a butterfly hairband in her hair and had promised Hazel any help in her maths homework, as long as she helped with their English comprehension. Patrick, on the other hand, had other useful skills. He was naturally confident, and could seemingly persuade other team members that giving their team more spaghetti and marshmallows was fair if he gave them some of Hazel's construction advice. So the team was complete: Hazel, project manager; Patrick, professional conman and Ayushi, calculations genius.

There were two classes in each year, N and H, named after the initials of the school, Newton Hall. Already, the class of 7N had decided that they were superior because they came first. 7H, of course, thought the opposite; alphabetically speaking they were first. Rivalry already had appeared and apparently was maintained for the rest of their school life.

It had been a long bus ride of just under an hour to the school. Hazel happily curled up on her coach seat and ploughed through her latest thriller book. This was the life for her; reading, sitting, no exercise. Sometimes Dad joked that Hazel was already a grandma, who just liked a quiet life. Hazel always smiled a secret smile. Perhaps her life looked quiet from the outside, but her books and active imagination more than made up for her non-sporty persona.

In the morning, they had an assembly given by the headmistress, who must have read every book ever published. Despite 'oozing power' as Hazel would later describe her, she wore a purple floral dress (Hazel approved) and had smiling eyes that keenly took in each of the new pupils sitting cross-legged before her.

Next, they had their class photos. Hazel, being one of the taller girls, was allowed to sit on the seven coveted chairs next to their teacher, Mr Barton. She twisted her pink shirt cuff round to hide a small mark of hot chocolate from breakfast time, making a mental note to blame Ella this evening if a teacher noticed the stain.

7N's first lesson was science. There were many "oohs' and 'aahs' as they entered the science laboratory. It was called the Perkins Lab.

'Why Perkins?' asked Ayushi boldly of the older sixth former who was their guide for the day.

'William Perkins was a famous chemist, who was renowned for the discovery of mauveine,' informed the sixth former with an intelligent flick of her pony tail.

'Amazing!' said Patrick. 'What an amazing discovery, definitely up there with my favourite top ten.' He paused and then added, 'For those who don't know about the amazing discovery of mauveine, could you tell them what it is? Ayushi is still confused, you see.'

Ayushi gave him an ice-cold glare. 'I had no idea you learnt such advanced science at your primary school, Patrick.'

The sixth former smiled patiently and explained, 'Well, Patrick, for the benefit of your new friends, mauveine was one first artificial dyes to be discovered. It is that lovely bright purple colour you see in Victorian dress.'

Wow, thought Hazel, could this school be any better! Naming a science lab after the very scientist who invented the colour purple. Now that was an achievement. She wrote the name, "Perkins" in her sparkly, purple note book under *Interesting People*.

Their first lesson, 'Safety in the Lab', surpassed expectations. A Bunsen burner was placed in front of each student, the most useful piece of science equipment they would meet in the laboratory. When connected to the gas supply through a long orange tube, this little metal chimney, only fifteen centimetres tall, would burst into flame with the touch of a lighted match. Then turning its collar would expose it to more oxygen, which in turn changed the orange "safety" flame to a blue mean menacing "roaring" flame reaching temperatures of over seven hundred degrees Celsius.

Dr Grey, a patient science teacher, who seemed more like a big brother than a science teacher as he looked quite young, inspected each pupil's flames in turn. He gave them a mark out of ten for their prompt setting up of apparatus. Ayushi somehow managed to set fire to the instructions, but luckily by the time Dr Grey came over to inspect their progress, all evidence of such tragedy had fortunately been burnt. Patrick lit his Bunsen burner with such practised flare that the teacher scribbled a mark, which to Hazel looked distinctly like eleven out of ten.

At the end of the lesson, they were awarded the homework of creating their own "Licence to Burn" certificates, which Dr Grey would sign next lesson.

Back in the playground, in the last ten minutes of the lesson, Hazel's tower had grown to Shard-like proportions. Other teams had turned to stare at its colossal stature. Mr Barton, sounded the final warning and all teams stepped back just in time to see Hazel's Eiffel tower turn into the leaning tower of Pisa before collapsing in a sorry state as if an invisible earthquake had hit Newton Hall.

'Oops!' apologised Ayushi. 'I think I made a mistake with my final calculation! I think I should have multiplied rather than divided.'

XxxxxxxxxxxX

Oak Academy

It was now or never.

Alice curled her cold toes on the edge of the diving board. She had been waiting all day for this one moment.

'Three, two, one, go!'

She launched herself forwards and kicked butterfly style into the surprisingly warm water. The water was soft and the pool had infinity-like ending so waves did not splash back from the edges. Much warmer than her local pool. The tiles were a lovely green colour and the mosaic of a dolphin was smiling at her from below.

There were six lanes. This was the first heat. If she was in the top three fastest times, she would go through to the final race, but then would need to be in the top two. She kicked and her strong arms propelled her forward. In the corner of her eye she saw her competitors not far away. There were two girls who were good. Yes, dangerous, Alice thought; they swam too quickly. It was four laps of the pool. Touch the side, come on, Alice! Already her muscles were beginning to ache. The other two dangerous ones were close on her tail, the remaining three swimmers were now half a lap behind.

Closing her eyes, Alice kicked harder. Arms moved faster. Whistle blew in the distance. 'Keep going, keep going!' Final touchdown. The three of them were in the running. One girl wore a pink shark swimming hat. Alice rolled her eyes; there always had to be one. The other girl looked blue with exhaustion. The sports teacher was checking the times, seemingly impressed, and beckoned over another teacher to check.

Alice hated waiting. As the second heat took place she wrapped herself up in a towel. She must remain warm, wishing to avoid that familiar feeling of cramp in her toes.

The digital times flashed on the board. After two heats, results were up. Alice's name was third. She was through to the finals. She looked up at the spectator stands. A few older kids were watching, they must have been in the senior teams. They were checking the times of the junior race and chatting with their sports teacher, Miss Striker. Alice took a deep breath. She closed her eyes and imagined her dad watching her. Not long now.

She stepped up to diving board three. She stared at the crystal green water below; she longed to swim into its warm depths again.

'Three, two, one, go!'

Finally, she leapt gracefully off the concrete platform and this time dived shallower, hoping to gain a distance advantage. As she surfaced, she imagined herself a dolphin dynamo and stretched her arms and legs to reach and move as far forward as possible. End of lap two and the three of them were close together again. The blue swimmer was splashing more now, her arms flailing rather than the controlled reach of the other, pink-shark-hatted girl. Final lap, there were two of them. The other girl must have tired, she had disappeared. All Alice could see was the final two hand strokes till the end. The end approached fast. She rapidly decelerated, avoiding smacking into the side. She whirled around and removed her goggles to squint at the red digital dashboard. But nothing was showing yet.

She removed her hat and lifted herself out of the pool, paddling her toes as she sat on the diving board, waiting. However, there was some commotion in the shallow end. The blue girl was being lifted out of the water. She was small and the sports teacher, Miss Striker, carried her with ease to the side. She was crying.

'Poor kid,' said a more senior sport Wasp, sitting next to Alice and Pink Shark Girl. 'She got a bad attack of cramp, had to stop. Though, if you ask me, she was going too fast though for her size, she needed to pace herself.'

The senior Wasp, called Crystal, got up and jogged over to where Miss Striker and the little girl were sitting. She gave her a large warm towel and handed her something in a Thermos flask to drink.

Alice and Pink Shark Girl cautiously went over to her. She still looked blue. Miss Striker was heartily patting her on the back and was telling her in a comforting tone how she would certainly be in the squad as third reserve.

'What's your name?' asked Alice.

'Tabitha, but my friends call me Tabby,' replied the girl, who was still shivering despite now being coated in four thick towels.

'Hi, Tabby, I'm Alice,' introduced Alice. 'Oh and this is Pink Shark—I mean—' Alice broke off, embarrassed. She hadn't known the other girl's name and "Pink Shark" had just tumbled out. 'Sorry!' She turned to "Pink Shark". 'It's just that you're a really good swimmer and your swimming hat has a shark on the front.'

To her surprise and relief, Pink Shark laughed. 'You don't recognise me?' She extended her hand in formal greeting to them both. The swimmer took off her hat to reveal her true identity and to Alice's amazement, she realised it was her cousin. 'I'm Miranda, but I guess I quite like the nickname Sharkie.'

'Miranda, Tabby and Alice,' said Miss Striker, 'Welcome to the Junior Wasp Swim Squad!'

There was a lot to sink in. Firstly, that she, Alice, had achieved her wish to be in the swim squad. Secondly, the fact that Miranda, "Sharkie", could actually swim really well and was quite nice about it, too. Why had she been so different at Marlows? Also, she wondered, was Jodie here too?

Crystal came bounding up to them, carrying large squashy packages. 'So, team, firstly, congrats. You each have a parcel, hopefully the right size. You each get special sports ties, you must wear them with your normal uniform. They show that you are part of the elite sports squad at Oak's. Secondly, here is your official swimming merchandise.' She waved a black swimsuit in the air, with a small logo of a wasp wearing goggles. Then she showed a yellow swim hat with "OAK ACADEMY" in black. Finally, she unfolded a large yellow hoody with "JUNIOR SWIM SQUAD" printed on the back.

'Team practice is twice a week, Monday and Thursday, four to five p.m. School competition days are Wednesdays, four to six. If you can't come, then your excuse had better be good. Oh, and my name's Alex, by the way. You are very lucky to be part of this team, young Wasps. Just remember, Miss Striker is the best teacher of the lot.'

XxxxxxxxxxxX

Friends made anything possible.

Alice, Tabby and Sharkie emerged from the changing room comparing their timetables. Oak Academy was a terrifyingly big concrete block of a school and therefore it was a mission to locate their actual classrooms. The first challenge of the morning was to go on a treasure hunt and mark off all the different rooms on the timetable. They had asked some of the older kids for help, but soon learnt that this was not always the best strategy. Each time they asked, they seemed to find themselves in the toilets, or worse.

To make the school feel less daunting, each girl was assigned a "family group" for half an hour each day.

This was like a class but was filled with three pupils from each year group in the school. The other newbie' as they were called in their first year, was a girl who looked rather street wise. She had large hoops in her ears and tried to chew gum (forbidden substance) at any available moment. The other girl seemed to know loads of the other newbies from her last school and thus decided it would be a waste of effort to spend time getting to know Alice. The twelve-year-olds in their family group were helpful about asking boring stuff like homework and teacher names. The thirteen-year-olds decided that school was ruining their chances of socialising and thus didn't inspire much enthusiasm. The fourteen-year-olds in the family decided that sleeping was the best occupation during family-time and therefore were a bit unresponsive to any questions. Finally, the oldest girls in the family were looking a little pale already for the start of term. Two of them woefully proclaimed that GCSEs were impossible and that they were already doomed to fail. The other, keener-looking one, happily told them that as long as they worked three hours extra per day from Year Seven, they would be fine.

One benefit of the modern building was that all the classrooms had glass walls. In the next classroom, apart from a small fight between some Year Eights. Tabby was day-dreaming out of the window. The classroom on the other side of the corridor was Sharkie's. She seemed to be interrogating the Year Ten, who was more intent on sleeping. At break time, she could easily find her new friends.

4. Fireworks

Winston's College

'Where r u?'

'By the Cndy Floss'

'Where r u?'

'Dodgems'

'Wait 4 me!'

As the term passed, the triplets spent more time apart. They no longer existed joined together as the 'Triple Trouble', as Dad used to call them, but more like 'just triplets'. It was Bonfire Night and luckily for the parents, only Ella's school, Winston's College, was celebrating. Apparently, Oak Academy viewed the idea of fireworks as a potential health and safety nightmare. Meanwhile, Newton Hall was too scared of angering the local residents with such a loud festive display.

However, things had gone wrong after the dodgems. Like all arguments, it had been a silly trigger which had initiated an explosion of sibling angst. Perhaps it had been bubbling up for ages, since results day in March. They had just come off the dodgems.

Hazel and Ella had thought they would be more successful if they teamed up to constantly collide with Alice's car. This had annoyed Alice more than they had realised.

'My school's better,' Alice yelled at Hazel and Ella as she pushed past them as they left the dodgems.

Alice threw her candy floss on the ground and grabbed Miranda. 'We're leaving, Sharkie. I can't stand them any more. They always think they're special just because they could choose where they went to school. Ergh, it makes me sick. Goodie, goodie Ella and her music snobby school and boring brain box, bookworm Hazel. Good luck in the real world. They won't find it easy from their privileged school bubbles.'

With regret, but to show solidarity, Miranda threw her toffee apple next to Alice's abandoned candy floss. They linked arms and marched with purpose in the direction of the Ferris wheel.

Ella had made a throwaway comment about how this was to be her last fun for the rest of the half term holiday, as she needed to revise for important exams when she returned. Hazel then contributed conversationally to say that at Newton Hall they had weekly assessments, "To prevent fuzzy brains".

'How about you, Alice?' asked Ella. 'Do they actually bother with exams at your school?'

'Maybe they only care about behaviour at Oak Academy?' thought Hazel aloud.

She was referring to the weekly emailed reports which Dad and Mum received about Alice's efforts. The academy put great emphasis on how each pupil was progressing and therefore sent a detailed spreadsheet on Alice's "class friendliness", "homework completion" and "class helpfulness". Her efforts were measured from one (illustrated by a super happy smiling emoji) to four (illustrated by a green crying emoji). So far, Alice was achieving one in sport and two in everything else. She laughed about it each week, but recently was getting more anxious about her siblings not reading the email. She didn't care, she told herself, Oak Academy just did things differently. To be honest, Mum and Dad rather liked this constant form of communication and wished Ella's and Hazel's schools did the same.

They hadn't meant to sound like they were "dumbing down" Alice's school, but that was what it felt like to Alice. She had had enough of them and their stupid "popular" schools. It sometimes felt to her that they were members of an exclusive club, which Oak Academy could never enter.

XxxxxxxxxxxX

The bench was lonely.

Ella and Hazel stared hopelessly in the direction of their disappearing shadows. Ella sighed and sat dejectedly on a nearby bench.

'Oops,' she said, shrugging her shoulders and absent-mindedly dropping her toffee apple on her wellington boots.

'Oh, cheer up, Ella.' Hazel sat beside her consolingly. 'It's not our fault she's got this chip on her shoulder.'

'I dunno,' replied Ella unwillingly. 'We probably didn't say the thing about tests in the right way.'

'Do you think she thought we were trying to gang up on her?' asked Hazel. 'I mean, it was just a question—' She trailed off as she contemplated whether the question was indeed fair. 'I wish we could just talk about it but we are always so busy, we rarely see each other so much nowadays.'

Ella thought quietly. 'Hang on.' She grabbed Hazel's arm. 'I've got an idea!'

'Eureka!' said Hazel. 'That's what scientists say when they have found something, it comes from the ancient Greek—'

'I have it!' interrupted Ella, 'Yeah, I know. We've just started learning Greek as well as Latin at Winston's and I really love it.'

'Hmmm. Latin is a dead language, as dead as dead can be, first it killed the Romans and now it's killing me!' laughed Hazel, quoting a well-known rhyme. 'What a strange fish you are, liking classics!'

'Well, Latin and Greek are musical, you see,' Ella tried to explain. 'They have conjugations and declensions, they have different vowel sounds and their sentences are logically constructed—' She tailed off as she noticed Hazel's attention waning. 'Anyway,' she startled Hazel by dragging her upwards, 'Come on, we're going to the Ferris wheel where Miranda and Alice are standing in the queue. It's our only chance.'

Hazel hoped that Ella's big idea was worth the effort of leaving the comfy bench and bounding like a mad bunny over to the fairground ride. As she half-heartedly jogged behind, Ella she wondered why someone would choose Latin and ancient Greek over the wonders of science.

XxxxxxxxxxxX

Something wasn't right.

By a strange coincidence, Alice, Hazel and Ella were all in the same Ferris wheel pod, looking down on the field of Bonfire Night celebrations below. Alice was fuming and deliberately staring in the opposite direction to her siblings so as to not catch their gaze. Cousins Miranda and Jodie, had been taken home by Auntie Bella, who had decided that the field was getting too dangerously muddy to stay for the fireworks themselves. However, as the three siblings were uncomfortably swaying in their pod, they noticed that the world stood still. More specifically, that the pod was no longer moving and they were suspended at the highest point on the wheel.

There were some concerned parents looking up at their stranded children, high up in the air. The fairground ride controller was shrugging his shoulders and doing little to calm the parents' nerves.

Ella looked down on the commotion. 'Looks like we've broken down.'

Alice rolled her eyes and pulled her hood over her plaited head. 'Great, just my luck, floating in mid-air on a freezing night with only you two for company.'

'Humph, charming,' retorted Hazel. 'For your information, Alice, it's not our idea of fun either.'

'Ha-ha, no. Silly me, you would rather be with more intelligent company, I suppose,' moaned Alice.

'Shut up, both of you,' snapped Ella. 'I can't stand it any longer. Even though we're sisters, triplets even, we never seem to see each other any more, and if we do spend any time together we argue and it's just—' Ella broke off mid-rant as a familiar beeping of ringtones distracted her.

'Are Yo 3 Ok?'

The pockets of the three sisters illuminated as a text message from Mum arrived simultaneously. Alice couldn't help but smile at Mum's attempt to abbreviate the message into "text speak".

'Wow, we should give Mum some lessons this half-term,' said Alice out loud as all three sisters peered out of the pod and saw Mum waving frantically below. Interestingly, Dad didn't look that worried and was happily looking after both Mum's and his mulled wine as she texted.

'Alive xxx', texted Alice grumpily.

'Cud u get me a hot choc wen we arrive. x', texted Hazel wishfully.

'Absolutely fine, don't worry! xxxx', texted Ella, trying to calm her agitated parent.

There was a silence and they looked to see Mum, squinting at her phone as she deciphered the messages of her daughters above.

'U are broken, but man says fine soon', Mum texted back informatively about the status quo of the broken-down Ferris wheel.

'K, x.', texted Alice.

'No worries, hot choc plz', texted Hazel.

'Luv u M & D!' texted Ella.

Apart from the rapid fire of text communication, the three sisters sat silently in their cold pod.

Ella started shivering. Alice rolled her eyes and handed over her woolly yellow scarf.

'Oh, thanks!' said Ella gratefully.

'One day,' said Alice, sounding slightly patronising, 'You will actually realise that it is better to be warm than look good.'

Ella blushed, but accepted the words as they were gratingly sensible. She wrapped the thick scarf three times around her neck and for once ignored the fact that the colour clashed with her pink puffer jacket.

'One day,' spoke up Hazel, who had suddenly thought this a good opportunity to begin a "sister talk", 'You will realise, Alice, that you are the best swimmer and general sportswoman in our family, and we don't get jealous of you. We don't mind that Dad drives you to lots of swimming galas each week, spending more time with you than us.'

Alice swallowed. The words had struck a chord with her. She had always taken for granted that Dad would be her "coach", kindly supporting her in each swimming competition. She hadn't realised that Ella and Hazel didn't see him as much on weekends as he was driving her to different swimming pools.

'Well,' offered Alice weakly, 'I wouldn't have minded if you had wanted to come with Dad and me when we drove to the races—'

However, Alice tailed off. She realised that she was fighting a losing battle. Her sisters had other interests. Just as she would have found listening to a music concert or going to a science lecture really dull, the same would be true of them for swimming.

Ella backed up Hazel's pep talk speech. 'We all choose to focus on our strengths. It gets a bit boring if we just moan about stuff we are not so good at.' Hazel nodded in agreement.

Ella gave a sigh and said, 'As the famous Roman poet said, *Carpe Diem*!' She stopped and then realised the effect of the words had been lost on her non-classically trained sisters.

'Okay, you were kind of making sense till you mentioned a dying carp,' replied Alice sulkily.

In the gloom of the dark sky and the coldness of their static pod, Hazel let out an amused snort. 'Ha-ha, dying carp! Trust you, Ella, to come up with some story about a Roman fish.'

Alice, despite her best efforts, began to laugh too and for the next minute they were in hysterics.

'No, no, no, you don't understand!' Ella blushed, shook her head and looked so desperately concerned that her two sisters muffled their laughter with their gloves.

'You see, the Roman Poet, Horace, used to say, *Carpe Diem*. It means "seize the day", not "dying carp"!'

'Oh,' said Alice. Then she couldn't help laughing again. 'I think "dying carp" is a much better phrase, it really gets one to appreciate life instead of being like a dead fish!'

Hazel roared with laughter and before Ella knew it, she was laughing with them too; it was fun to be silly sometimes. Magically, the Ferris wheel began to move. There was a universal cheer from the huddle of concerned parents below, who were delighted that their children would not be frozen overnight after all.

After receiving a giant bear hug from Mum and Dad, Ella crept over to the fairground operator.

He stood with a smile on his face and asked her in a quiet voice, 'Well, miss, did your plan work? I had to stop it for ten minutes and you wouldn't believe how annoying some of your parents were getting. You will have to buy two additional tickets to get over my stress of being so hassled by those troublesome parents of yours. Also, some parents may not trust me to operate the ride for their little darlings, so that extra money will come in handy.'

This was a cheeky request by the ride operator, as the minor glitch had resulted in the increased popularity of the Ferris wheel. Other students now viewed the ride with additional excitement due to the potential risk of getting stuck.

Ella dug in her pink puffer pockets and found the requisite money. She felt a little sad as it meant that she would have no treat money left for the rides, but that didn't matter. Her clever plan to stop the Ferris wheel so that she and Hazel could have a talk with Alice had worked. Besides, Alice owed her a toffee apple anyway.

'Come on, Triple Trouble,' said Dad. 'Time to go. Mum has had too much mulled wine.'

Mum poked Dad affectionately in the ribs. 'Hmmm, thanks, Robin. I suppose you just drank the children's apple juice cocktail, did you?'

Dad laughed and put his arms round the five of them. 'Well, did we have fun?'

Alice, Ella and Hazel smiled at each other in a secret silence.

Alice broke the silence first. 'Best Bonfire Night ever!'

5. Ballet Magic

'Is ballet boring?'

'Um...how long is it?'

'U 2 r so uncultured'

'Where r we going nyway?

'Come on, you three, breakfast time!' Mum called from downstairs in a demanding voice.

Alice, Ella and Hazel emerged from their warm beds unwillingly. It was no longer just Hazel who found getting out of bed a struggle; the other two girls were starting to appreciate the benefits of a lengthy morning lie-in.

Mum appeared, cup of coffee in hand, at the door. 'Hazel,' she addressed her daughter, who unfortunately was still under the bed covers. 'If we miss the train because of you—'

'Why am I always the one who is blamed!' angrily retorted Hazel. 'Alice and Ella aren't ready either, yet it is my fault again!'

Mum's voice softened. 'Well, they have made more progress than you.' She pointed to the other two, who were half dressed between them, causing both of them to look smug.

Half an hour later, the Platt family were walking cautiously down the road. It was a bit icy and Ella had decided that her new sparkly party shoes would be the perfect choice to see the ballet in Birmingham. She smiled at them proudly, though her toes were feeling the frosty weather and Mum kept on shooting disapproving glances at the decidedly un-hardy footwear choice.

'Are we walking to Birmingham, Mum?' asked Hazel, who clearly thought they had walked for long enough already.

'Luckily for you, no, we are not, we don't want to miss the ballet in the afternoon. We are taking the train from Euston.'

Hazel was happy. Trains pleased her. No exercise, sitting down and reading. Perfect!

XxxxxxxxxxxX

The Train

The Platt family were lucky.

Their efforts in walking the entire length of the train to find an empty row of seats paid off and now they had two table seats opposite each other. Hazel sat down, still muffled up and produced a new library book from her puffer jacket pocket. Dad carefully laid down the assortment of hot drinks, ordered in a last-minute dash before boarding. It had been freezing outside and Ella gave a warm grateful shiver as she took her slightly spilt hot chocolate cup.

Barely had they sat down, before the ticket inspector arrived.

'No phones, please, miss,' he said in a warning tone at Alice, who had unwisely decided to text Miranda a status update of their weekend adventures.

'Oh, sorry,' replied a guilty Alice, who was conveniently sitting under the "No phones allowed. Quiet Coach" sign.

Now it was Hazel's turn to look smug. It always was reassuring when another family member was told off apart from her.

Alice saw the look and made a mental note to hide Hazel's book later in revenge.

'So, we will arrive in Birmingham at 11.55 and first spend half an hour only in the new shopping centre above the station,' began Dad, who always enjoyed being the voice of authority for such trips. 'Then *The Nutcracker* begins at two, so we will have a quick lunch nearby.'

Ella gazed happily out of the window and day-dreamed as she watched the moving countryside. She was super excited. Two things close to her heart; the first thing was shopping and the second was to see a show with music. She had heard about the *Nutcracker*, of course. It was the ballet to see. The orchestra playing were one of the most famous, Miss Wood had told her and as she wanted to get into the youth orchestra next year, maybe she could pick up some tips. Unconsciously, she began to drum her fingers on the table to an imaginary tune.

Alice adopted her latest strategy of texting under the table. She had dimmed her screen so it made the glow from the phone less obvious. Miranda was taking the trials to get into the Under Thirteens' County Squad this morning and Alice wanted to know every detail. Did Alice like ballet? Well, the only similarity to swimming was that the ballerinas wore leotards which were sort of the same as swimsuits. Actually, she was quite happy going to Birmingham for the day. She had been training hard at swimming recently and had been saved from the usual five thirty a.m. Saturday start today. She could do with a rest. She lay back and closed her eyes.

'Mum?' asked Hazel slyly, thinking back to the successful phone call that she had eavesdropped on all those months ago. 'What was it like going to school with Auntie Bella?'

'I guess that my school days must be too boring to ask about,' chimed in Dad, trying to sound as if he had been forgotten.

'Ha-ha, was there even school when you were a boy, Dad? As you are so old!' teased Alice.

Ella looked concerned for a moment but then in her usual way of trying to pour oil on troubled waters, she answered, 'Well, Dad, you were an only child, you see. Mum had a twin sister, her school days were more similar to ours than yours—'

'Humph,' said Dad and then resumed reading his rather good crime thriller by his favourite author, secretly glad that he could read without being disturbed.

Mum put down her newspaper and chewed her reading glasses in an absent-minded fashion, as if she was deciding how much to tell her daughters.

'Well, Auntie Bella and I went to different schools,' Mum began.

'What!' exclaimed Alice. 'Completely like us, you mean?'

'Pretty much, except we were twins rather than triplets,' Mum corrected.

'So who went where?' asked Hazel, who had been desperate to know the truth ever since the overheard phone call between Mum and Auntie Bella last year.

'Oh. Well, it doesn't matter really, does it?' said Mum.

'It does to us!' piped up Hazel.

'Hmmm,' warned Mum as she picked up her reading glasses again and found the article she had been reading. 'Remember, you three, curiosity kills the cat!'

XxxxxxxxxxxX

Dad was happy.

The train arrived perfectly on time and the family disembarked onto the bustling train platform. Loads of cafes and shops filled the entrance hall. Upstairs, there was a familiar department store, brand new and boasting its new wares and Ella walked with purpose towards the upwards escalator.

'Race you, Ella!' shouted Alice. The two of them hurtled towards the moving metallic staircase. Alice was certainly the fitter of the two in the pool. However, Ella had the additional training of walking up several flights of stairs every day to reach her classroom, or tree house as it was affectionately known by the students, and thus had a spring in her run. Hazel happily left them to it and decided that escalators were the perfect rest stop to read a page of her gripping new book.

Ella went straight up the stairs and looked around for the shoe department, her next love after music. Alice meanwhile headed for the sports section to find new swimming goggles. Hazel found a nice comfy-looking sofa in the furniture area and curled up just like Tiger on the train and settled down to read. The parents looked at the three triplets heading in their different directions and sighed. How they were related to each other was a mystery.

After rescuing Ella from the shoe department, they squeezed through crowds of keen shoppers to the Christmas market in the centre of the town. It was as if they had arrived in Lapland. There were log cabin lookalike stalls selling all sorts of Christmas goodies. Ella saw a musical glockenspiel box, which chimed *Silent Night* beautifully. Hazel was intrigued by the copper candle holder which when lit, caused the stars and angels on the ring above it to spin around as if they were flying in the sky. Alice, meanwhile, was keen to try skiing on the digital ski slope. The parents grabbed the German equivalent of hot dogs, called Bratwurst, for them all to eat as they explored the market covered by artificial swirling snow.

As they made their way to the theatre, they passed a street of old-fashioned shops. Much to the triplets' delight, the final shop was a traditional sweet shop.

Dad looked at his watch; they had fifteen minutes till the show began. He looked at the expectant triplets and rolled his eyes. 'All right then, Triple Trouble. You have precisely two and a half minutes to equip yourselves with two ounces of sweets each.'

The three sisters whooped and hurtled in to the shop; the parents were amused to see even Hazel move quickly. A middle-aged lady behind the counter welcomed them into the dark shop, made more realistic by no electric lighting.

'Well, my dears, off to see the show? What can I get you today?'

'Umm—' Alice, almost the boldest of the three, spoke first. 'The parents said we could have two ounces each of any sweet, but how much is that in modern English?'

The lady laughed and explained that the weight was equivalent to two small chocolate bars.

Hazel was content with the news and decided to order quickly. 'Could I have the sherbet lemons, please? Could you make my portion a generous two ounces?'

The other two triplets thought this an excellent idea, to test the two ounce rule generosity.

'Could I have a very generous portion of strawberry fizzy laces, please?' requested Alice.

'And could I have an extremely generous portion of aniseed balls, pretty please?'

XxxxxxxxxxxX

The Theatre

Ballet was not boring.

The curtains plummeted down gracefully as the ballerinas in the *Nutcracker* bowed for a final time. Ella had loved the orchestra and the presence of a choir had added the magic touch. Alice had been inspired by the dancers' graceful moves, which were remarkably like a swimmer doing an elegant crawl. Meanwhile, Hazel enjoyed poring over the show programme to learn about the different ballerinas' biographies. She had even completed a tricky crossword competition to gain a backstage pass to the ballet performance. She had posted her entry in a giant gold Christmas tree in the interval and was keeping her fingers and toes crossed for the end announcement.

Katie Platt smiled at her children. They were so transfixed by the performance they had forgotten to ask for the requisite ice creams in the interval. The costumes still sparkled in their memories. Clara wore a beautiful white nightgown and the Sugar Plum Fairy shone in her pale pink tutu sprinkled with diamonds. Katie made a mental note to tell her now good friend, Bella, to book it for her two daughters, Jodie and Miranda, next year. It was just too good to be true.

As the seating lights brightened and the audience slowly found their bags and coats, Dad made a sign for them to hurry up.

'Come on, Hazel,' he beckoned impatiently. 'We don't want to miss the train going home and there are loads of people here to beat us to it.'

'Oh, Robin, don't worry so much. We don't have to move like clockwork, you know,' replied Mum, supporting Hazel's unhasty movements, much to Hazel's surprise. 'We can always get the next train.'

Hazel smiled at Mum but remained seated. 'Just wait a mo',' she asked pleadingly. 'They are going to announce the crossword winner at the end of the show.'

'Oh, Hazel,' Mum addressed the girl sympathetically. There are hundreds of people here. There is probably more chance of you winning the lottery than that competition.'

'Now there's an interesting thought,' chirped Alice. 'Mum, can I buy a lottery ticket?' I am feeling particularly lucky today with all this Nutcracker magic?'

'No,' said Mum and Dad in synchronized agreement.

'And now, ladies and gentlemen—' There was a drum roll as the actor who had played Drosselmeyer appeared from behind the stage curtain, 'The Nutcracker Christmas Cracker competition had a winner. Are you the lucky one out there?'

The audience excitedly took their seats and all three sisters crossed their fingers.

'Hazel Platt!' roared Drosselmeyer.

There was a large sigh from the audience as they realised they were not the lucky ones. However, in Row D, there was a happy chorus of cheering from Alice, Ella and Hazel.

Hazel couldn't believe her luck. 'Wow! I never win anything! Gosh, this is completely unexpected.'

'Ha-ha,' snorted Alice. 'Anyone would think that she had won a lifetime achievement award or something rather than just a crossword competition.'

Drosselmeyer beckoned the Platt family to come onto the stage. Mum was blushing and Dad was looking a little annoyed because they were certainly going to miss the planned train now. However, as he saw the delight on Hazel's face, he decided to relax and enjoy the 'behind the scenes' experience.

For once, Hazel was the first in the family to lead the way onto the stage, as there was a background of gentle applause from the now-leaving audience. Drosselmeyer opened the thick red velvet curtain and they suddenly found themselves next to the giant

Christmas tree lit by candles, with lots of ballerinas looking rather tired, stretching their limbs on the spiral staircase.

Ella was in seventh heaven, admiring several sparking costumes hanging by the large mock fireplace. She loved the Flower Fairy's costume of a pearlescent tutu with a pale pink and darker fuchsia-coloured shirt. Alice was entertained by the stronger male dancers practising lifting the females. Much to her astonishment, she herself was suddenly lifted into the air and spun around by the evil Rat King.

The best part was still to come and Drosselmeyer pointed to the huge white swan covered in feathers which had transported Clara to this magical kingdom. The swan was gliding from the ceiling via a concealed zip wire to where Hazel stood.

'Fancy a ride?' he asked her with a twinkle in his eye.

Hazel couldn't believe her luck. There was squashy cushioned seat inside the hollowed-out swan and two handles for her to hold on. There was a sharp tug on a powerful rope by the Rat King and before she knew it, she was suspended mid-air, looking down on her family who were gaping in astonishment. The Rat King whirled her around the entire stage and then made her land with a rather exciting nose dive back onto the stage.

'Wow! I filmed the entire thing on my phone,' said Alice excitedly. 'Please can I have a go, too?'

Fortunately, the Rat King and Drosselmeyer were very good natured and duly allowed Alice to try out the flying swan too. Each sister took it in turns to film their journey into the stage set skies twice.

The sisters then watched, mesmerized, as each played the recording of their flight back to them.

'Come and have a look, Ella,' said Hazel distractedly. However, as they turned to where they thought Ella stood, they saw a small ballerina instead, who had been watching them in amusement. 'Oh, where has she gone?'

At that moment, they heard the sound of a tuneful melody from down below in the bowels of the stage, where the orchestra sat. In the middle of the orchestra stood the conductor, a small, balding chap with greyish wispy hair and dressed still in his black tie. The surrounding seats were now empty apart from a lone violinist wearing a pink puffer coat.

'Ella!' shouted Alice. 'How did you get down there?'

The little violinist looked up at her two sisters, who were watching impatiently.

The conductor flicked them away with his conductor's baton and commanded Ella to continue. Alice beckoned to Hazel to take the stairs to the orchestra pit below.

The melody was beautiful, Hazel recognized it as *The Dance of the Sugar Plum Fairy*. The playing was beautiful too, but surely it could not be Ella? She wasn't that good.

As both sisters emerged from the pit, they were surprised to see two other spectators there too, Mum and Dad. They were sitting hand in hand smiling proudly. There in the centre was the "Little pink puffer jacket violin-playing virtuoso", as Alice would later describe her.

The playing stopped and Mum and Dad burst into applause. Hazel and Alice joined in a little belatedly and Ella, amazingly not blushing, took a practised bow.

'Not bad, Maestro,' called out Alice. Then she whispered to Hazel, 'But if you ask me, I would say it was showing off a little to just start playing in the middle of the stage.'

Hazel chuckled, 'Yeah, but you've got to admit, she did sound rather good. In fact, there seemed more depth to her playing this time, I wonder what has changed, is it the acoustics in here?'

Then it was Ella's turn to explain. 'I said I loved playing the violin and I got a music scholarship to Winston's and the next thing I knew, the lead violinist gave me his instrument to try.'

'It was beautiful, darling,' praised Mum as she wiped a small tear from her eye. 'Your practising really seems to have paid off.'

Now it was the small but imposing conductor's turn to address the small audience. 'You are good for your age,' he said in a rather pompous-sounding accent. 'I shall send you an invitation to try for the Youth Orchestra in London. You must audition next year.'

Ella's ears burned. This was her dream come true. That orchestra were amazing. Normally they only accepted children over the age of thirteen, so if she got in—just imagine what Miss Wood would say if she was successful in the audition!

Thirty minutes later, having waved good bye to their ballet friends, they emerged into the now dark square, feeling distinctly more festive than when they had arrived. They slowly made their way back to the train station, following some other late theatregoers like obedient sheep. The triplets were deep in argument about which character would be the best to play. Ella liked Clara as she was the important one, as the story was all about her. Alice loved the Rat King, because she claimed it was always more fun to play an evil person as they had a more interesting character. Meanwhile Hazel chose Drosselmeyer, the great magician, as without him, the whole spectacle could never have occurred.

After ending the argument by agreeing to disagree. The three sisters gratefully flopped onto their train seats. Within five minutes, Ella and Alice fell fast asleep, dreaming of the presents they hoped Father Christmas would bring them tomorrow. However, their dreams were short lived when there was an unexpected interruption.

XxxxxxxxxxxX

'Is this seat free?'

It was a harmless question but one which often causes annoyance to the person asked. Hazel felt rudely awakened from her reading happiness. She instinctively wanted to say no; she was happily curled up on her window seat with her back slouched against the welcome empty seat. However, as she glanced upwards she saw a girl of about her age, with dark curls, carrying a large purple container with a wire mesh front. The girl had an intelligent look about her, and Hazel was pleased to see that in her free hand she was carrying a book by one of her favourite authors.

Hazel graciously sat upright and smiled. 'Yes, as long as you don't mind being neighbours with my sisters Alice and Ella.'

The girl grinned. She had a naturally naughty look about her and winked. 'Nope, I don't mind. As long as you don't mind sitting next to a baby bear.'

Ella stopped day-dreaming, Alice woke from her power nap, Hazel's book dropped to the floor with a clunk. The parents were deep in discussion about something boring and hadn't heard this alarming statement, so continued their boring conversation.

The girl took their astonished silence for approval and sat down next to Hazel, placing the purple container on the table. All three girls looked nervous but Alice was the most curious.

'Well, where's the bear?' asked Alice directly.

'In here,' smiled the girl, tapping the roof of the purple container. At that moment, there was a distinct sound of moving paws from the box and the girls saw what looked remarkably like a bear but in miniature form.

The girl laughed. 'Well, it was funny to see the shock on your faces. Okay, so he isn't a real bear, but I am sure he must be related. He is called a Bernese Mountain Dog, traditionally a breed of dog from the Swiss Alps. He has loads of fur to keep him warm.'

Baby Bear was the most adorable dog they had ever seen. His body had a generous coating of dark brown fur with light brown fur around his legs. His dark eyes were surrounded by lighter brown fur rings and he had a white bib of fur down his middle as if he was wearing a smart dinner jacket. His paws were playfully soft and when he opened his mouth to pant, he seemed to give a big smile instead. His tail thudded in his carry cot to symbolise he was delighted to have so many new friends as company on his train journey.

Now that the danger had passed, having safely ascertained that the bear was not a real bear, Ella peered into the puppy's cage. 'Oh, he looks sweet. What's his name?'

'He is nameless,' replied the girl. 'My auntie breeds this type of dog at her home in Birmingham and I just visited her for the day. She gave this 'baby bear' to give to a special vet in London to find him a home. His owners will name him.'

'Can we play with him?' asked Alice cheekily.

The girl curled her already curled hair in her fingers as she thought deeply and then said, 'Okay then, but take care as his paws are a little muddy. I took him for a walk in the park before boarding the train.'

For once, even Ella didn't mind that her carefully chosen clothes were at risk of being a little dirty. Baby Bear, as he was nicknamed, was a huge success and they spent a happy hour playing pass-the-parcel with him on the train.

Dad looked up from his gripping crime thriller, feeling pleased that he had almost finished it. It was a door stop of a book and Mum had been telling him off for ages as he hadn't had time to read it. Mum looked up too and smiled. The three triplets were happily spending time with one another again as they played with Baby Bear. Dad suddenly had a mad thought that they could adopt the little dog. No, no, too much to think of, having three eleven-year-old daughters made life busy enough and the little dog would soon turn into a very big dog. They certainly didn't need another family member.

'Bye, Baby Bear!' yelled Alice as they disembarked onto the hectic platform at Euston Station.

The three triplets turned to wave at the little girl and say farewell to their new-found friend. Ella was sure that Bear had woofed a goodbye and tried hard to fight back the tears which had suddenly welled up. She didn't want to leave him. He was their friend, but more than a friend; he almost felt like a member of the family.

6. Ice Breaker

'We r so old!'

'Hppy bday golden oldie!'

'Go 2 slp'

'No. Whoop! Party!'

Hillside Ice rink

Mum was right.

The ice rink was penguin shaped. Beside it, supersize polar bears were dancing under igloos, but it was freezing. Alice wished she had worn a hat as Mum had suggested. She glanced jealously at Ella and Hazel, who had followed their mum's advice and were sporting large woollen rainbow hats. She shivered and skated faster, deliberately lifting her skates off the ice and thus appeared to skate aggressively but was simply trying to keep warm.

She felt a friendly slap on her back and Miranda was suddenly trying to rugby tackle her to the icy floor.

Alice giggled, 'Stop, you muffin. You are scarily strong, Sharkie.'

It was true. Miranda had returned from the Christmas holidays having grown about six inches. This certainly gave her a competitor's advantage in the pool. The two had always finished their races within centimetres of each other, but now Miranda won by a convincing half stroke. She was also part of the Under Thirteens County Squad and the extra practising certainly seemed to be paying off.

'Where's Jodie?' Alice asked her friend.

Miranda looked around and saw Clara and Jodie attempting synchronised skating. It was a bit lopsided as Jodie was rather smaller than her partner in crime and as a result their skating direction was always a little haphazard. Clara saw Alice and gave her a friendly wave. Well, it was her birthday and it was all classroom politics in Year Seven; the more people you knew, the more parties you were invited too. Of course, the other side of the coin worked nicely too; the more people who came to your party, the more presents you got.

Hillside ice rink was playing host to the triplets' twelfth birthday party. They had invited over thirty people. Well, three different schools was an opportunity for quite a few friends. Mum, Dad and Bella, now miraculously friends, were sitting huddled in the ice café which overlooked the rink, looking content with their warming cappuccinos. Astrid had her noise pressed to the window. The closest she got to sport was her daily trumpet practice; any other exercise was a pointless waste of energy in her eyes. She had been given a double chocolate muffin and was drumming her fingers to an invisible melody as she happily munched away.

The luminous orange ice marshal blew his whistle, signalling the end of the triplets' power skate session. Alice in a burst of energy zoomed towards the exit barrier. Unfortunately, the synchronised skating duo, Jodie and Clara, had the same thought and the three collided on the ice. There was a crunch. The ice marshal looked down at the three girls. Confused, he decided to blow his whistle again. Now everyone on the ice rink was staring.

Alice was hauled up by Miranda. She was as strong as she looked. Miranda then did the same for her twin, who was desperately trying to hold back the tears. Miranda finally hauled up a surprisingly quiet Clara, only to be rewarded by a sickening yell.

'Noooo! You idiot!' Clara shrieked hysterically. 'I've done something to my leg, it's killing me. Oh, it's all your fault.'

Now this was hardly fair as Miranda hadn't even been involved in the collision. At that moment, Mum, Dad and Bella appeared.

'Mummy!' yelled Jodie, then proceeded to burst into tears. 'They've ruined my party.'

Miranda looked at her scornfully, 'It's not your party, muppet, it's the triplets'. Besides, it could be worse, you could be Clara.'

'Miranda,' scolded her mother, 'What a thing to say. Clara can't help being Clara!'

Miranda shook her head, everyone was telling her off today for completely no reason. 'No, Mum, you don't understand. It's because Clara can't stand up.'

'Oh.' There was a unified note of anxiety in the three adults' voices. They looked at the blond-haired angel girl (though of course appearances were deceptive) on the floor and felt that usual worrying sinking feeling in their stomachs. What would they tell her parents?

XxxxxxxxxxxX

North Central hospital

They should improve daytime TV.

The triplets, plus Mum, Dad, Bella, the twins and Clara were in A&E. Although they had only been waiting fifteen minutes, to Alice it felt an eternity. Clara was still whimpering, even though she was beginning to realise she was gaining little sympathy. Jodie was now bored and so had gone off to the gift shop to buy herself a present. Ella looked a little pale. Maybe it was the smell or the drama but she wasn't keen on hospitals. Miranda had fallen asleep and was quietly snoring. It was only Hazel who looked happy.

'Dr Brunel will see you now.' The waiting party looked up to see a small nurse with glasses and clipboard pointing at a small consulting room. Mum and Bella wheeled Clara into the room, while Dad stayed with the others. At the last moment, Hazel came bounding up too. She was intrigued; the hospital

85

was like a giant science lab and the doctors wore their white coats like true scientists. She liked it.

'So, young lady,' the young male doctor addressed Clara in a friendly manner, 'What has brought you to my hospital?'

Before the "young lady" could speak, Hazel chimed in. 'Suspected fracture of the left leg resulting from a three person collision on the ice rink. Patient is unable to weight bear and is supposedly in considerable pain. The symptoms would suggest the tibia is broken.'

Mum and Bella stared at Hazel, too shocked to warn her for being a little over-confident.

The young doctor smiled. 'Well, well, we have a prognosis from our medical student here, but now we must be sure with an X-ray. We always need medical evidence.'

Clara seemed perkier, having received some well-deserved medical attention and said in a warm voice, 'I agree with Dr Hazel.'

Hazel beamed with pride and felt rather proud of this out-of-character response from Clara. Perhaps, she thought to herself, the fall had not only broken her leg but also her pride. Dr Brunel scribbled something unintelligible on his clipboard and summoned the efficient-looking nurse to take them to the X-ray department.

XxxxxxxxxxxX

Hazel's future was decided.

Back at home, Mum, Dad, Alice, Ella and Hazel were sitting down around the kitchen table. It was funny to think how the time had flown. Their tastes for drinks had changed too. Alice was partial to fruit smoothies, Ella now loved a cup of tea and Hazel enjoyed a hot chocolate with whipped cream dusted with cocoa powder. In the middle of the table sat the masterpiece that was their birthday cake. To celebrate the occasion of the ice rink birthday party, it was an ice cream birthday cake in the shape of a large circular ice rink, with three little plastic penguins, one wearing a pink hat, another a purple hat and the third a green hat.

Their experience at North Central hospital was thankfully already becoming a distant memory. Clara's mum had rushed to pick up her daughter but was bemoaning the fact that she would have to buy some new skirts to fit over the plaster cast of her broken leg. Clara perked up at this idea of extra shopping. The girl had changed in personality from being a little too self-indulgent, to a more interesting "patient old sport" as Alice complimented her.

Hazel had left the X-ray department elated with joy. Dr Brunel and his X-ray friend had described in detail the workings of the medical machine and also the healing process of fractured bones. Hazel had discovered her dream career of the future. She was going to become a doctor.

7. Freedom

'I hv ure lunch, don't like the marmite sandwich.'

'Oops, I ate ures already, cheese bagel ws quite tasty'

'Wat!! U 8 mine! It's only 9am!'

'I got 2 kit kats, Mum must love me the most, lol!'

Trips meant no lessons.

It so happened that all three of the triplets' schools had picked the same day for their end of term trip. However, destinations were as different as the sisters' personalities.

XxxxxxxxxxxX

Ella

Ella liked the tube at rush hour.

All the serious business people rushing up and down the escalator with a look of importance in their eyes, wearing smart suits and speedily emailing on their smart phones. Their sense of urgency was addictive. She wanted to work in the city to share this buzz of action.

'Come on, Astrid, we'll lose the others if we don't hurry.' Ella yanked her friend affectionately, who had unwisely decided to pause at the new cafe on the platform at Westminster tube station. Astrid patiently let herself be led by her impatient friend and cast a farewell look at the brownies and assorted muffins through the window.

At the far end of the platform, Clara and Jodie were both staring at their new phones in intense concentration. Though they were best friends, they spent a lot of time not talking to each other, but instead playing the latest version of a virtual game, in which they competed against each other to make the most successful fashion empire, called "Fash-i-own". They gave Astrid and Ella a salutary nod, as they joined them. They all got on much better after the fall, as it became known. Clara had made a quick recovery from her broken leg and was much nicer for it. Astrid and Ella liked them better but still found them both rather dull and thus they all rubbed along all right.

Miss Walker was wearing a hi-vis jacket and looked stressed, as teachers had a habit of looking every time they took a class outside the safety of the classroom. The luminous jacket was a little unnecessary, thought Ella, seeing as they were all nearly twelve years old and perfectly able to take a tube alone. They boarded the District Line train to Wimbledon. Ella naughtily swung from the bright green handles in the carriage; they were the perfect height for monkey bars. Astrid grinned, but sat on a seat near the phone friends, Jodie and Clara. Miss Walker signalled to Ella to stop and told her to sit beside her. Glowing red, Ella sat down and pretended to immerse herself in the *Championships* book that she had found at home. It informed the reader all about the tennis championships at Wimbledon.

As they stopped at the various Green Line tube stations, Ella thought about her sisters embarking on their trips. Alice would have loved this trip; Wimbledon was all about sport. Ella was not sporty and was secretly jealous of Alice's marvellous hand-eye coordination. It was stupid to feel jealous, though, thought Ella. Alice had never been jealous of Ella's violin playing, or had she? Alice was now in the Under Thirteen School Squad and she had upcoming county trials. Ella loved her sister obviously, but conversation was often boring as it just revolved around sport, or sporting events and sporting personalities.

Alice loved her school, too. Ella shivered, never a day passed when she did not feel relief that she had been accepted by Winston's. She often passed some of the older Oak Academy pupils, on the walk back from school, and they looked at her maroon uniform as if she was public enemy number one. She saw some of the junior kids at the bus stop beating each other up; the adults waiting for the bus pretended not to see. Alice wondered if they were actually scared. Alice never spoke badly about Oak Academy. She was gifted by turning potentially scary stories of bad behaviour into funny ones at dinner time. Though when Alice had told of a new teacher on playground duty having sweetie wrappers stuffed in her coat hood, not a particularly funny story at all!

Then there was Hazel. Completely different again, total book worm. Just as Alice was never happy unless she was playing sport, Hazel was never happy unless she was learning something. Her sister's obsession for almost the whole school year had been science. She loved it. She loved the "purple lab", as she called it, the experiments, the white lab coats. She never stopped talking about the lesson that her favourite teacher (science of course) Mr X had given them. She pored over her science homework till the early hours of the morning.

Alice and Ella had joked that Hazel must know the whole Periodic Table with over a hundred elements by heart. Hazel sometimes went too far though in her work. Occasionally Ella caught Mum and Dad shooting concerned looks at her sister as she had dark rings under her eyes. It was a strange thought that parents would prefer their child to work less rather than more, but sometimes Hazel lost track of time. After the incident with Clara on the ice rink, Hazel's love had turned to being a doctor. Alice made her blush whenever she mentioned that she only liked medicine because Dr Brunel had been so good looking.

Just then Clara let out a groan. 'Oh, that is super annoying. Such a nightmare, my phone has died.'

As was often the case with the new sophisticated smart phones, the battery life was remarkably poor. Jodie gave her a sympathetic stare.

'Oh, no, you were making such a successful Fash-i-own. I loved the purple leather shirt with sequined colour you had created. I forgot my back-up charger, total disaster!' replied Jodie.

Astrid smirked and Jodie then proceeded to ask the rest of the carriage if they had a back-up charger.

'Southfields,' the train driver suddenly remarked on the tannoy system. 'Change here for the England Lawn Tennis Club.'

Miss Walker zipped up the hi-vis jacket and beckoned them all onto the pretty platform outside. There were trees and flowers carefully planted and little tennis rackets showing the direction to the Tennis Club.

XxxxxxxxxxxX

The Court

Ella wanted to be a ball girl.

The class walked past the Ball Distribution Office, where a long line of ball boys and ball girls were queuing to collect their ration of tennis balls for their assigned court. There were about twenty courts and the children – well, hardly children, thought Ella, they must have been fifteen years old – looked happily cool despite the heat. They were dressed immaculately in a navy-blue uniform of polo shirt and shorts with bright white gym shoes, all of which bore the unmistakable crest of a well-known fashion designer.

'Ooh, Clara!' whispered Jodie excitedly. 'We must use today as inspiration for Fash-i-own! Wow, who knew Wimbledon was so cool, I thought only old people worked here!'

'Totally brilliant,' agreed Clara. 'Let's have a selfie with your phone, so that we can show our mums this evening.'

Miss Walker rolled her eyes at the fashion-conscious duo. 'Come on you lot, this is a busy place and we need to get to the hill to see the tennis. After all, we didn't come to Wimbledon to shop!'

This time, Ella, Jodie and Clara all looked disappointed. After music and Latin, shopping came next on Ella's list of favourite things. 'Oh, I am sure the gift shop here is amazing,' sighed Ella.

Jodie and Clara made similar groans of agreement.

Miss Walker led the slow walking class towards the Hill. The large mound of earth which gave a birds-eye view of the whole of the club, had been called by a number of different nick names, always based on the current English number one player. The most recent player had just retired and so the hill was just called "the Hill" for the present.

They sat in front of a large digital screen, almost twenty metres wide. It was projecting the match play from Centre Court. Two men, a Russian and an American.

'I bet a bowl of strawberries and whipped cream, that the Russian wins. Who is willing to take on my bet?' asked Astrid bravely.

Ella rolled her eyes at her funny friend. Quite to her surprise, however, half the class, were willing to take on Astrid, and accepted her bet.

Ella glanced down the Hill towards the practice courts. There was a small white tent, where players sat between matches and if they were feeling generous, could sign autographs for keen fans. The word "autograph" actually derived from the ancient Greek word, "auto" self and "grapho", I write. She loved knowing the origins of words, not that anyone would actually listen to her. Alice just called her a show-off.

Jodie and Clara were already networking, as they liked to call it and had managed to collect three signatures already. Ella stretched her crossed legs out and skipped down the stairs to join them. She made it into the latest selfie photo with Jodie, Clara and a young British junior player, who looked decidedly sulky.

At that moment, there was a tumultuous round of applause and the Hill seemed to erupt with spectators. The match had ended and the fans were packing away. They walked up the Hill as the tsunami of spectators were walking down and there amongst the crowds sat a contented Astrid. She had won the match, or rather, the Russian had won the match. She was surrounded by over a dozen bowls of strawberries and cream.

'Ha-ha,' laughed Ella. 'You will certainly achieve your five a day today, Astrid.'

Astrid chuckled. She was good natured and extended three large bowls of strawberries and cream to Ella, Clara and Jodie.

'Perfect,' Clara accepted gratefully. 'The ultimate Wimbledon selfie photo! Smile!'

XxxxxxxxxxxX

Alice

'Dreams start here!'

The neon block capital letters were the size of Alice. They stood in the atrium of a large glass building which towered towards the sky like a rocket.

Miss Striker had taken her swimming school team on a well-deserved "sports treat". In fact, the treat was nothing to do with sport; sometimes she thought it best to broaden their horizons and make them think of life outside the rigours of exercise. They were in the headquarters of a company which had made one of Alice's favourite childhood toys, "Model Me".

The idea was simple: to create miniature models of your family. All you needed to do was send in a photo of your family with their ages and key personality types. Then, two weeks later, you would receive your "mini me"; your family (only a few inches tall). You could order them a place to live, clothes, friends: then you created your dream world as you could play with them, as you wished.

Alice studied a large mirror with interest. There was a sign above it which just said, "Look into your future".

At first, Alice looked at Alice. She was smaller than her friend Sharkie, but that wasn't too difficult as she was a good few inches above the average height of the class. She was the tallest out of Ella and Hazel and was proud. As silly as it sounded, it made her feel like the oldest triplet. In reality, she actually was only two minutes older than Ella. As it was a trip day, the class had been allowed to forego the burden of school blazers and thus she just had a yellow shirt, half tucked into her black pleated polyester skirt. Alice's hair was tied in a high pony tail. Hazel preferred a neat plait and Ella liked her hair to flow over her shoulders, so she wore a silver hairband with a bow. It was funny to think of her sisters as she stared at herself in this mirror. They didn't only differ on the outside, but they also differed inside too.

Hazel was clever. Yes, it was true she went to a "brain box school" as Alice described it, but she was clever there, too. Her exam grades were sparklingly good. This was impressive, considering the average class mark was often eighty-seven per cent and Hazel received "Exceeds Expectations", which meant that she surpassed this mark easily. Yet, she didn't ever seem big-headed. Alice would have made sure that she never became an insufferable know-it-all, but Hazel never seemed to notice her peculiar genius. She was just too intent reading, revising for the next test, preferring to do puzzle questions than watching TV. Weird.

Then there was Ella. Half the time, the girl didn't seem real. Was she in danger of becoming too materialistic? Hazel thought that she had been spending too long in the company of Clara and Jodie recently; their heads seemed only filled with shopping and phones. Yet at least, these were only hobbies for Ella. Her true academic loves of music and Latin made her more interesting than her classmates. What would Ella decide to be when she was older? Would people remember her for her violin playing? Would Hazel always be introduced as, "Ella's sister – the violin player, you know".

'So, young ladies. Welcome to Model Me!' A young chap dressed in a bright canary yellow shirt and purple tie appeared from behind the tall mirror which Alice had been staring into.

'You must be super excited to be here, I know you love it already. We are going to be great buddies!'

The class rolled their eyes as they listened to the patronising speech.

'Yo, buddy, where are the loos?' asked a tall girl with earring hoops. She was a fifteen-year-old swimmer, Crystal, who certainly didn't go out of her way to make new friends.

'Oh, my name is Inventor Jasper, young lady,' corrected the blushing Jasper. 'The loos are just past the imagination fountain under the escalator.'

'Oh, soz,' replied Crystal. 'I thought your name was Buddy.' Crystal and two of her closest mates sauntered over to the loos, laughing.

'Be quick, girls,' shouted Miss Striker. 'We've got an action-packed day ahead here.'

As the crew of the three girls proceeded to walk as slowly as possibly to the nearby toilets, Jasper turned back to the rest of the swim squad and pointed to the mirror. 'Well, let's begin with our newest dream, right here, right now.'

The rest of the squad gasped. One moment, the mirror had shown a picture of Alice, life sized, an image captured just a few seconds ago and then the mirror glowed green. A calendar had appeared at the top of the mirror. The dates were flying around Alice and suddenly it was one year later. Alice was thirteen years old. She looked a little taller (shown by a height chart in the background), her hair had been cut short but other than that, the same.

'All you've done is stretch her a bit,' said Miranda. 'That is basic trick photography, I could do better on my phone.'

It was Jasper's turn to laugh, he was in control of their curiosity appetite. 'Okay, what about Alice in Year Ten? The same age as—' Jasper broke off to point at Crystal and her friends re-emerging from the bathroom, having applied a thick coating of make-up.

'Err—oh, Crystal,' prompted Miss Striker helpfully.

'Thanks, Miss,' replied Jasper. 'The same age as Crystal.'

The mirror glowed green again and the virtual calendar began to turn again. The class stared. Alice had grown about six inches. She wore a hair band, her eyes were a deep turquoise blue and she wore a silver charm necklace. She looked pretty.

'Not bad, Alice,' smirked Crystal. 'Not as fit as me, but good start.'

Alice blushed. However, before she could tell Jasper to stop his digital time-turning magic, the mirror glowed and the calendar began to turn again and before she knew it she was eighteen years old.

Her hair was more blonde than brown; perhaps the chlorine in the swimming pool was responsible for its gentle bleaching. She wore a thin black hair band, she had grown a fringe, and wore a blue and white tracksuit, looking elegantly athletic. There was a red ribbon around her neck which held a small gold medal. But what was the medal? There was no detail, even though Alice desperately squinted in vain.

'Ooh, nice trainers, Alice!' whispered Tabby.

The class roared at the remark. Jasper seemed content with this response. 'Ha-ha, yes, well predicting fashion trends in the future is a creative business, you know. Glad you like the trainers though, our fashion inventors will be happy. Follow me, all, stay close and don't touch anything unless you want to turn into a two-inch plastic creation of yourself!'

As they went up the spiral escalator, a weird concept in itself, Tabby made dutiful notes on the whole experience. There were three different "inventors" at Model Me. The dream inventors (including Jasper) were responsible for coming up with the next big idea as to what children wanted in a toy. Life inventors were then responsible for making that idea happen as a new model. Finally, the fashion inventors would extend the life of the new model so that it could be a success for as long as possible.

Model Me was bizarre.

In the Creation Zone, (also known as the room for modelling dreams) the class sat on luminous space hoppers grouped around low lying tables. The tables had little pools of modelling clay and the class spent an enjoyable few minutes making models of themselves and their families. Then Crystal and her mates spoilt the fun by starting a modelling clay snowball style fight.

Predicting mess and mayhem, Jasper moved then swiftly on before their creative juices became too "active", as he described it. He took them down a marble corridor, to a large glass window overlooking the manufacturing of all the new "mini me" families. Smiling, he pushed a button and the floor beneath the class disappeared.

Crystal screamed and grasped her friend, who looked equally taken aback.

'Keep your swimming hat on, Crystal,' replied Miss Striker unsympathetically. 'It's a glass floor, you are not going to fall through.'

The rest of the team laughed, but not too much as the junior ones were still a little scared of Crystal in the pool. They bent down and saw the millions of little robots carefully piecing together new family members.

Lunch was a little too futuristic for Alice's liking. They were led to a canteen, and sat down wearily on bean bags, which were actually filled with a liquid gel, making them sway like a boat on a rough sea. Then they were each handed an iPad. Based on a series of random questions, such as, "Would you rather adopt a lion or a penguin?" and, "Would you prefer a bright orange house or a bright pink house?" it then produced a lunch menu.

The lunch popped out from a concealed flap on the table. Alice received a turquoise blue soup (apparently, blueberry porridge), a glow-in-the-dark orange drink (carrot and ginger juice) and a multi-coloured ice cream triangle (actually cold white chocolate). However, she preferred Miranda's menu and she was good natured enough to swap. Thus in the end, Alice tucked into a lime green yogurt sundae (mashed up potato and peas), a red smoothie (strawberry and grapefruit ice cream) and a chocolate bar shaped as a fish (which fortunately was simply chocolate).

'Come on then, team, we'd better get moving,' sighed Miss Striker, who was also a little confused by the futuristic meal.

'Hang on there, Miss Striker,' said Inventor Jasper cheerily and he tapped the side of his nose. 'I haven't finished with your kids yet!'

He led the way to a small room, called the Power Room. There, the chairs were attached to pedals, which you had to cycle like a bike to turn on the lights in the dark room.

'Now, girls, they don't call me a dream inventor for nothing, you know.' He pushed a small button and out of the air, a small parcel fell into the laps of each of the students.

Crystal was the first to rip open the metallic wrapping paper of her small box. She stared as if she couldn't believe her eyes, 'OMG, that is well fit!' Crystal was admiring a twenty-two-year-old version of herself. She wore a patent leather jacket, holey jeans and a lot of "bling" as she liked to describe it, finished with a designer handbag slung across her mini shoulders.

Jasper almost jumped for joy at such praise of the gift. 'Well, they are rather cool! We decided to make "mini mes" of all of you but in seven years' time! Our cameras were tracking your every move and decision today, so we have hopefully created a realistic picture thanks to our life and fashion inventors.'

The class all opened their mini mes, fascinated in their future selves. Miranda and Alice put their mini mes side by side. Alice was intrigued that she was taller than Miranda. The eighteen-year-old Miranda looked less sporty and was looking surprising smart in a pair a black leggings and dark denim tunic dress with a pearl bracelet.

'What about you, Miss?' asked Crystal, seemingly innocently.

'Now, now, Crystal, I am old enough already, thank you,' replied Miss Striker. She had received a small metallic parcel too but had firmly locked it safely in her handbag, away from the curious eyes of her swim squad.

'All right then, team, I have an idea,' interrupted Miss Striker from their day-dreaming at their future selves. 'Team photo. Put your mini mes on the table here, and we will take a team photo in the future. One, Two, Three, Cheese!'

Perhaps thanks to Inventor Jasper or the strange lunch menu, Alice had extraordinary dreams that night. She had carefully put her mini me on her dressing table by the side of her bed. Its small tracksuit-wearing form was wrapped up in her yellow swim hat for a duvet. She smiled proudly at the little eighteen-year-old Alice. All she could think about, over and over again, was the happy question: in seven years' time, why would she have a gold medal?

XxxxxxxxxxxX

Hazel

Science solved crimes!

Hazel decided she had chosen the right subject to be good at. Inside a large lecture theatre, she, Ayushi and Patrick were listening spellbound to a university professor, who was happily explaining that science created the most exciting jobs in the world. They had been invited to attend a science CSI Olympiad, in which they had to compete in a series of science challenges with other Year Seven school pupils.

Professor Wright wore a long white lab coat and had just carried out an impressive array of demonstrations. 'Science is the best career in the world. From being a doctor to creating the next chocolate bar, from designing new life changing medicines to detecting dangerous explosive devices, from navigating blind to working out how a crime had been committed. Science is omnipresent, everywhere! Its name comes from the Latin word for knowledge.'

Hazel made a mental note to tell this to Ella, though she probably already knew. The room was packed with pupils from ten different schools across London. Hazel wore her Newton Hall uniform of navy skirt, pink shirt and golden tie with pride. Unlike many other twelve-year-olds, Hazel loved her uniform and sometimes given half a chance would have been happy to wear it on the weekends too.

On reflection, Hazel had more in common with Ella than Alice. At least they could agree that Alice was bonkers about sport. Ella was sometimes a little annoying when she was determined to practise the same line of music for an hour until she achieved the correct rhythm. However, she understood that Hazel would not share her love of watching TV programmes about famous musicians and therefore didn't force her to watch them, whereas Alice would force them to watch every sports programme imaginable. Ella seemed more grown up than Alice and Hazel though. She cared about her clothes all the time, never got too flustered and was polite to their parents' friends, even the boring ones who gave terrible presents like XXL T-shirts (too big, unless they used them as nighties) or "thank you" cards (annoying as you always had to write a "thank you" card to them).

Hazel could never understand how Alice enjoyed the sheer brutality of her early morning swim regime; how she could rise out of bed at five thirty a.m., knowing that a hundred laps of the cold pool awaited.

Then the horrible feeling on competition day, when you were wet and freezing, standing by the pool, competitors looking fierce, treating each other as enemies. Neither could she share Alice's love of watching sport. It was too predictable. Four laps of the pool, fastest time a winner, end. Four hundred metres sprint over the hurdles, the steeplechase which went on forever, but what was the point of going round and round—

'Now for my final demonstration, elephants' toothpaste!'

The pupils leaned forwards expectantly in anticipation.

'I think I need a volunteer—' the professor stopped and smiled. The whole of the lecture theatre had raised their hands, even the teachers.

Dr Grey took pity on the desperate Hazel, who had raised both of her hands in the air.

'If you stand up, he will certainly pick you,' he said to her quietly. Hazel smiled and stood up; she was never easily embarrassed.

'What are your favourite colours, Hazel?'

Hazel considered this for a moment and then remembered Alice and Ella. 'Pink, that's my sister, Ella. Green, that's Alice, my other sister's favourite. Oh, and Purple, that's my favourite colour and it was synthesised by William Perkins when he was only still a student.'

A girl in a grey uniform with white shirt turned around and muttered, "Goodie goodie!"

Patrick gave her the evil eye and Ayushi darkly wrote down the school name in her note book. 'We'll need to remember our enemy,' she whispered as menacingly as she could to Hazel.

'Ha-ha!' exclaimed the professor delightedly, having not heard the "Goodie goodie" incident. 'Spoken like a true scientist. What a great chemist Perkins was indeed. Okay, so pink, purple and green—' He picked up the different coloured dyes and added them to the measuring cylinder.

'Now in this large cylinder, we have an interesting mix of hydrogen peroxide (turns your hair blonde, ladies, but beware as it is rather powerful oxidising agent). We also have a catalyst (makes reactions go nice and fast) and finally, it is toothpaste, so I thought we would add some washing up liquid.'

Patrick pressed "play" on his video phone.

Professor Wright was a magician. The very moment he added the final ingredient, the catalyst, a tower of foam erupted from the measuring cylinder. To the students' delight, it did indeed look just like toothpaste as the foam had a swirling pattern of pink, purple and green. It then fell into spirals which surrounded the measuring cylinder like an exotic snake and plumes of smoke extruded from the bubbly mess.

'Cool!' shouted Patrick, impressed by the experiment. 'Could you do it again but add more of the catalyst?'

'Well, actually it's hot stuff!' corrected Dr Grey. 'You see, that reaction is called an exothermic reaction. It gives off heat.'

'Let me get my phone, I want to time the rate of reaction in comparison to the last trial,' whispered an excited Ayushi to Hazel. 'Then I can draw graphs to clearly show the difference in reaction times.'

Dr Grey turned a blind eye. The students weren't meant to have their phones with them on a trip, but as long as there was a science-related excuse, he supposed it was all right.

Hazel cautiously filmed the second experiment of elephants' toothpaste, she was sure even her sisters would find it fun.

'Hands up, who thinks the reaction will be more exciting?' asked Professor Wright. About half the students put up their hands, including Hazel and the rest of 7N. 'How about slower?' About a third of students put up their hand this time, including the girl who had been mean to Hazel. 'Who thinks the reaction will be the same?' The remaining few students cautiously lifted their hands mid-way as if unsure of the question.

The professor laughed, threw twice as much catalyst into the cylinder and stood back. The tower of foam shot out of the measuring cylinder at twice the speed as before and there was an impressed round of applause. Hazel noticed with satisfaction that the mean girl had been incorrect and her ears were glowing red as she realised her mistake.

'Well done, those who predicted the reaction would occur twice as quickly,' announced the professor as he shot the class of Newton Hall a congratulatory wink.

Dr Grey looked distinctly proud of his budding young scientists. 'Now, can anyone tell me why?'

Hazel's hands shot into the air again, but the professor was keen to allow a greater audience participation. His eyes settled on Patrick.

Patrick smiled smugly and said in a loud confident voice, 'Because a catalyst speeds up the rate of the reaction. Everyone knows that! Well, everyone clearly apart from the school sitting below us, who thought it would slow the reaction down. I think they need to do a little more chemistry revision.'

There was a babble of nervous giggles, apart from Heatherfield School below. Their science teacher, a serious lady with thick grey-framed glasses, turned around and fixed her thin unsmiling eyes on Dr Grey.

'Oops,' said Ayushi quietly to Hazel. 'I think we have just made our first enemy in the competition. We definitely need to win now.'

XxxxxxxxxxxX

The Lab

This was proper science.

All the pupil competitors had put on pairs of goggles, which had a cool fluorescent green rim, and white lab coats with the university crest. Hazel smiled at herself in the reflection in the glass window; she almost looked a professional research chemist. The lab was surrounded by orange fume cupboards, which as the name suggested, were simply cupboard-shaped boxes, which had sliding glass lids for dangerous experiments so that the toxic products could be sucked harmlessly away by the extractor fan.

Then the whole lab was divided into layers of white benches, which hosted an assortment of science equipment. Patrick looked keenly at the rotary evaporator, which was a glass, round-bottomed flask, whirling its contents violently so that all the water could evaporate. Meanwhile Ayushi had been delighted in finding a UV-vis spectrometer which was a large white box with computer attached, and on the screen graphs of every colour were being generated.

Their task was to become forensic scientists, special chemists who solved crimes. The crime today was simple: someone had stolen Professor Wright's favourite Bunsen burner and they had to assess the evidence to find out who had done such a terrible deed. First, they had to decipher a code, using a mini Sudoku, and work out the initial message.

'Whoop, whoop!' said Ayushi, 'I knew Sudoku existed for a reason other than saving me from boredom on car journeys.' She happily grabbed a purple biro and immersed herself in the art of deciphering the numerical message.

Patrick smiled encouragingly, 'You know, one day, you will make a great spy, Ayushi,' and Ayushi considered this briefly and nodded.

Unfortunately, Newton Hall students were placed next to their arch enemy school, Heatherfield. The mean girl and her so-called friends were staring at the number coding puzzle, perplexed. Hazel saw her whisper something to her closest friends and they smirked, walking away. Infuriatingly, the Heatherfield students were always wandering around the lab, looking for lab equipment which they seemingly were missing.

'I know what their game is,' whispered Patrick. 'They don't know how to answer the puzzle so they are cheating. Look, each student is copying down a line in their note book.'

Hazel felt herself getting annoyed, yet this encouraged the group to work faster. Ayushi found a spare lab coat and safely hid the code solutions underneath.

'Come on guys, what's the next task?' asked Patrick, who had decided to be project manager for this challenge.

Hazel read the instructions. 'Oh, good, we get to use my favourite technique, chromatography.'

'Always the mark of a true scientist to have a favourite technique,' said a familiar voice and standing above them was Professor Wright, looking with interest at Ayushi's code. 'Do you know the name comes from the Greek words, "colour", and, "writing"?'

Hazel noted this down as another titbit of classical information that her sister Ella would approve of. Hazel was an expert at the technique, she had even performed a class presentation on its science, for extra homework. The concept was simple. Cut a small rectangular piece of filter paper and dot a small spot of coloured ink about a centimetre from the bottom. Then, suspend the filter paper in a beaker containing a small amount of water, careful not to touch the ink spot, otherwise that would dissolve into the water. Then, wait just a few minutes for the ink spot to rise up the paper (carried by the water). Then, the ink separates into its different colours (green splits into yellow and blue), creating a beautiful rainbow effect on the paper. Different inks will create different patterns, so you can compare them and work out which is most similar to the standard ink in question.

So the riddle was simple. The school that had stolen Professor Wright's Bunsen burner had left a ransom note in a purple coloured ink. Now there were lots of different purple pens to analyse and the one which had the closest pattern to the actual note was the crime scene pen.

'So, first we need to carefully perform chromatography on the actual pen and see what pattern is produced. Then we can do separate chromatography on each of the suspect pens and compare, to see which pattern is similar to the actual pen.'

'All right, Sherlock,' laughed Patrick but then said in a serious undertone, 'but take care as the enemy are looking.'

The next half hour flew by and they had just completed their purple pen experiments when there was a disturbance. One of the Heatherfield pupils was lying on the floor with her eyes closed.

'What's happened here?' boomed the voice of Professor Wright. 'Do we have a poor unfortunate student who has been harmed during this crime scene investigation?'

At that point, the student worriedly opened her eyes. 'I felt a bit faint, Professor,' whimpered the girl.

'Oh dear, how terrible!' said the professor, sounding concerned. 'Well, you must go home immediately and forsake your team members, the goodie bag and the celebratory crime-solved cake at the end.'

The girl was clearly miserable at hearing such news. 'Oh no, Professor. I think I am feeling a little better now. Maybe I will just sit down a while to recover.'

The professor smiled to himself; he had dealt with many drama queens in his time. He sadly shook his head and replied, 'No, no. You must not trouble yourself, my dear. I am sure your team will tell you all about the rest of the event tomorrow. We can't have you sitting down in the lab, you must stand up when you are doing experiments, I am afraid.'

The girl got up rather quickly, looking annoyed. She glared at the Newton Hall team, as if it was their fault. Hazel felt uncomfortable. The whole incident had been odd; something wasn't right. Ayushi, Hazel and Patrick returned to their allotted lab bench.

'What!' Patrick exclaimed. All three of them froze and looked at the disaster scene. Their bench had been flooded in water and all their beautiful evidence, their purple chromatograms, had been drowned, their distinct patterns washed away.

'Sabotage!' yelled Patrick and turned to face the smirking team from Heatherfield.

'What a shame,' said the mean Heatherfield girl in mock sympathy. 'There's no way that you can win now that all your evidence is washed away and we only have five minutes left.'

Patrick was fuming. 'It was a set up. The girl fainting was just a distraction while one of their other evil team must have sprayed water on our bench. I can't believe it.'

Hazel groaned; there was no way that the professor would believe them either. Besides, it sounded a bit tell-tale-like when you tried to explain.

'Can I tell you a secret?' Ayushi interrupted their moaning. To their surprise, she was smiling. Out of her lab coat pocket she took out her carefully concealed smart phone. 'I took photos of each chromatogram. Now we compare each photo in turn to work out which purple pen was guilty.'

'We're saved!' cheered Patrick and Hazel in unison.

'Our physical evidence may have been destroyed but we have created virtual evidence instead!' said Patrick proudly.

'Time's up!' cheerily shouted the professor. 'Submit your results to the Chemical Crime Solving Office here.'

XxxxxxxxxxxX

The Finale

The audience was restless.

Ayushi, Hazel and Patrick were sitting nervously in their seats. Hazel noticed that Dr Grey was also looking keen to know who had one.

'You've got to beat Heatherfield,' he muttered under his breath. Patrick grinned to himself. While the students had been busy solving crimes, their teachers had attended a "science network coffee session". The networking between Dr Grey and the Heatherfield science teacher had clearly not gone well as they were looking daggers at each other, as Hazel described dramatically.

'In third place is—drum roll please!' shouted the professor over the students, who were forgetting to be quiet in all the excitement. 'Round of applause to Heatherfield!'

Interestingly, apart from Heatherfield, the whole lecture theatre was hushed to a cold quiet. It was only Heatherfield that clapped themselves. Word had got round that they had cheated and no one wanted to be associated with their school.

'You lucky team,' continued the professor, oblivious to the cool reception. 'You receive a DVD all about the periodic table!'

There was an enthusiastic smattering of applause from their science teacher but no one else.

'Now in second place—' The professor paused for dramatic effect. 'It is the Summer Hill team!' A warmer, louder applause broke out. At least that team had seemed nicer enough and hadn't cheated.

'Well done, Summer Hill! You receive an inflatable rubber ring decorated with all your favourite elemental symbols!'

'Finally, the winners—' The professor stalled the audience again. Dr Grey crunched his knuckles subconsciously. Patrick chewed his fingers, Ayushi chewed her hair and Hazel closed her eyes.

'Congratulations, Newton Hall!' roared the professor.

Dr Grey leapt up and gave each of his budding scientists a high five.

'Dr Grey is so cool,' whispered Hazel to Ayushi, who nodded in agreement.

'What's our prize, Professor?' cheekily asked Patrick.

The professor smiled as he revealed their silver, gold and purple test tube trophies made out of a shiny metal. Each test tube was engraved with, "Mini Professor of the Year!"

'You will have to decide amongst you, who gets which colour,' added the professor, as Hazel snatched the purple one happily. Patrick was pleased with gold and Ayushi decided that silver was most sophisticated. 'You also get your own pair of glow-in-the-dark lab goggles and a university lab coat too!'

Hazel was delighted. She immediately put on her new lab coat and the professor laughed. The lab coat was about six sizes too large and it made her look a little like a small white marshmallow.

'Trust me, my dear,' called the professor to a lab-coat-swamped Hazel. 'In a few years' time, when you are ready to go to university that lab coat will fit perfectly.'

8. Sports United

'I h8 2day.'

'Whoop, I can't w8'

'Hehe, I'm in the band, c u l8r!'

It was a prime picnic spot.

Bella waved at Katie Platt. 'Yoo hoo, over here, my dear!'

Bella had clearly snuck into the sports ground early. She had managed to steal the best location on the whole running track. She sat on a sloped bank, under a small cedar tree with a generous-sized cashmere rug and a large hamper. Its site offered the perfect combination of sunshine and shade; not to mention, if you wished, a birds-eye view of all the races on the running track beneath.

'Well thank goodness, all three schools finally saw sense and decided to have a shared sports day this year,' sighed Katie Platt, as she gratefully sat on the soft rug, placing her smaller hamper to one side. She glanced down on the large track and squinted to spot her three daughters in their various locations. She smiled as she witnessed Alice dedicatedly jogging on the spot to warm up for her first race. At the finish line, the band started playing and sure enough, there was Ella, happily sitting next to Astrid, playing a familiar tune on the violin. Finding Hazel was trickier. She was certainly not looking forward to sports day and would be trying to expend as little energy as possible. No, no sight of the little bookworm yet.

XxxxxxxxxxxX

Alice

Alice tucked her phone into her money belt.

She plugged in her iPod and began her warm-up stretching routine. Sharkie was in a similar zone of preparation. Both were excited and thought today was the best day in the school calendar. Yes, there were no lessons, but what made the day great was the fact that it was a hundred per cent sport. If Alice was a headmistress, she decided she would have sports day every Friday, then it would seem like a three-day weekend. Win, win!

Oak Academy was based in the centre of the track. They were the largest school to be taking part. Sports day only included the first two junior years of the school (Years Seven and Eight), but that meant over four hundred pupils for the Academy. A group of enterprising Year Eightss were trying to sell their half-melted chocolate bars for twice the price to a bunch of gullible Year Sevens, one of whom was their good friend Tabby.

'Oh, when will she learn!' exclaimed Sharkie and strode over to rescue the poor unsuspecting Tabby. It was certainly a good nickname for the girl as she was surprisingly gifted at acting like a little kitten and falling prey to more menacing older Wasps.

XxxxxxxxxxxX

Hazel

Hazel congratulated herself.

She and her good friend, Ayushi, between them had managed to be assigned "third reserve" for only two races. According to the super brain of maths genius Ayushi, this meant that they only had a one per cent chance of being selected to actually compete in sports day proceedings.

In a small patch of sunshine, safely away from the gaze of their sports teacher, Miss Field, the girls settled down to read. Their sports bags were not filled with clothes but books, of course. Hazel had brought a large compendium of cryptic crosswords and Ayushi had a large Sudoku and Mensa puzzle challenge magazine. Patrick, their other school companion, actually was rather good at sports, so they had decidedly to temporarily abandon him for the day. He didn't mind, his brain was focused on the games themselves. He and his other sporting friends were determined to beat the other two school teams participating. All race winners were allotted points and the school with the most points at the end was awarded the Tri-School Cup. It was the first year of this multi-school tournament and Newton Hall were desperate to win.

XxxxxxxxxxxX

Ella

The Orchestra of Sports tuned slowly.

The band was made up of the three schools; however, fortunately for Ella and Astrid they were seated together. Astrid looked up at the blue sky contentedly. She opened her violin case and slid a secret compartment to one side to reveal an impressive selection of sweets: sherbet lemons, strawberry laces, toffee eclairs and tasty sour cola bottles.

'Hmm—...' Astrid said pensively. 'I'll have to begin with the softer sweets, otherwise the strong heat from the sun will turn them into a strange-tasting unified jelly of flavours.'

The pair of boys behind them from Oak Academy tapped Astrid on the back with their bows. 'I will trade you a pack of crisps for eight sherbet lemons,' offered one boy in a business-like tone.

Astrid's eyes gleamed, considering the possibility. 'If you include a bottle of fizzy apple juice, the deal is done,' she answered, matching the tone.

The boy smiled, handed over the demand and ruffled his already ruffled hair. 'The name's Hugo, by the way.'

Astrid returned her side of the treat deal and then resumed talking to Ella without further acknowledgement of Hugo or his friend. Ella smiled. Astrid was effortlessly cool and didn't need any more friends.

At that moment, the music master from Winston's gave the signal and the Orchestra of Sports began their first recital, *Chariots of Fire*.

XxxxxxxxxxxX

Hazel

Sudoku had its limits.

Hazel had soon tired of the crossword, Sudoku, Mensa challenge and left Ayushi still deliberating over a complex mathematical puzzle. She had seen a large white marquee with an ambulance parked next to it and was intrigued. As she approached the tent she saw the sign, "First Aid" and, determined to expand her medical knowledge further, lifted its entry flap to observe the goings-on.

There were five temporary beds. Three were occupied by students. Two of them clearly knew each other as they were shouting unfriendly comments. Both were Oak Academy students; Hazel recognised the little wasp logo on their yellow sports T-shirts. The smaller girl was clutching an ice pack to her nose but it seemed to be making little difference to the dark red flow emanating from the chilled area. The other girl was whimpering as she tried to flex her fingers straight. 'I want my mummy!' she yelled.

A young chap entered the tent. He was wearing an immaculate white lab coat with a stethoscope dangling from his neck. He grinned at the three patients and then turned to Hazel, who was still examining the scene with interest. 'I know you, mini doctor.'

Hazel, glanced up in surprise and was amazed to see a familiar face, 'Dr Brunel!' she exclaimed. 'I remember you, too!'

It already seemed ages ago since that fateful party in which Clara had broken her leg. Though on reflection, every cloud had a silver lining and Clara had become much friendlier since. Dr Brunel had bandaged her leg and explained the workings of the X-ray machine to Hazel so patiently and he was here now! Sports day was suddenly bearable again!

XxxxxxxxxxxX

Alice

Adrenalin surged through her veins.

Alice stood on the starting line in Lane Two. Sharkie was in Lane One. The other lanes were occupied by Winston College and Newton Hall pupils. The students made no attempt to pretend to be nice to each other. They were enemies on the track. There was only one winner after all. Fifteen hundred metres – just under four laps of the track – and all would be over.

For the last fifteen minutes, Alice had deliberately avoided Miranda. She had made the excuse to go to the toilet and had walked incredibly slowly towards the changing rooms at the far end of the sports ground so as to have a few minutes in peace. It was difficult having a friend like Sharkie. She was so good at what Alice wanted to be good at. Yes, Alice knew that her own swimming and athletic performance had improved this year at an impressive level. However, Sharkie's had improved even more. It wasn't fair. Alice was trying harder, she knew it. Yet, Sharkie still had the edge. She towered more than four inches taller than Alice, which gave a significant sporting advantage.

Every night, Alice wished she would wake up having had a surprise growth spurt. At least she was taller than Hazel or Ella, but that didn't matter as neither was particularly sporty; they didn't need to be tall. Miss Striker had told her that everyone grew at different times. Besides, just being tall didn't make you a great athlete.

Miss Striker blew the starting whistle, the runners started forwards, the whistle blew a second time with authority: stop. False start.

Sharkie muttered something darkly to Alice. Alice pretended to laugh but hadn't heard the comment. The Winston's college pupil was blushing. She had false started, apparently – tripped over her shoe lace. Alice took a breath. Back on the line. Ready, deep breath.

The whistle start blew. In the distance, Alice heard the Orchestra of Sports play a well-known film tune. Ella must have been playing in the band, she was good now. Too good. Focus, Alice, she told herself.

The first lap, there were four of them. The false start girl hadn't recovered from the embarrassment and had decided to pull out of the race. The other boy from Newton Hall stopped only halfway round as his new phone had fallen onto the track and he was determined to save it, rather than have his digital social life temporarily ruined.

Alice gritted her teeth and accidently bit her tongue. The iron taste of blood flooded her mouth; she spat it out, not wanting to choke. She guiltily looked at her yellow polo shirt, now slightly flecked red. Annoyingly, Sharkie was running well. She was pacing herself, she was incredibly fit and didn't seem like she was expending too much effort. The other Winston College competitor was good, too, also a swimmer. Alice recognised her from the inter-school swimming gala last term. She had beaten Alice and what was worse, she clearly remembered her victory as she smiled at Alice in a distinctly unfriendly way.

The other competitor was from Newton Hall. He was tiring, too unfit. Why was he even running in the race? It seemed as if he was already having breathing troubles. Alice wanted to yell out to warn him to stop. He didn't look well.

Two laps down. The Newton Hall boy was turning purple. Sharkie was a foot ahead of Alice. Meanwhile, the Winston College girl was running almost on top of Alice. She could hear the girl breathing. Irrationally, Alice thought she was deliberately stealing her oxygen. Alice felt shamefully puffed already, why was she so unfit in relation to the others?

The horn gave the dreaded signal of the final lap. Alice's muscles ached. Sharkie was at least two strides ahead. Alice looked up at the blurred spectators, trying to find her mum, but she was moving too fast, it made her dizzy. There were just three of them left; Alice didn't want to look back. Half a lap, the Winston's College girl was speeding up, she almost seemed to be chuckling as she approached Sharkie. Yet, she was running too close.

Quarter of a lap remained. Sharkie turned and saw this girl come up beside her. They were both deliberately vying for the inside track, the shortest distance to run. They were millimetres away from —

Suddenly, Alice was alone. She wanted to stop to make sense of what had happened. She wanted to look back to see that Sharkie was all right, to see where both girls had fallen. However, the crowd was roaring, it gave her no choice. She had to complete the last few metres, the sole competitor on the track.

XxxxxxxxxxxX

Then she saw them.

Mum was there. She was standing up, clapping her, clapping Alice. Ella was waving her violin bow, seemingly having given up playing the music. Hazel was on the finish line with someone in a white coat. Hazel was actually jumping up and down, screaming something inaudible at Alice. Hazel never expended energy unnecessarily. She had to finish.

The finishing ribbon gently lassoed her stomach. The horn sounded. Miss Striker was shouting the result into the loud speaker. Hazel gave her a bear hug. Ella waved her bow in encouragement. Mum gave her the thumbs up. Miss Striker gave her a high five. She had won. Alice had won. It was a nice feeling. She remembered watching the Olympics a few years ago, they must feel a hundred times what I am feeling now, she thought. She felt like she could sprint the fifteen hundred metres again, just running on pure happiness. Wow, for once, she wasn't the second best, she was the best.

Bella appeared, looking worried. Guilt then descended on Alice as quickly as happiness had arrived. On the track, Miranda and the Winston's College girl were busy untangling themselves; they were not best friends.

'Now, now, Miranda, it was only an accident,' Alice heard Bella say to her fuming daughter. Miranda was not calmed by such gentle logic and stormed away to where Jodie and Clara were giving the Winston's college girl the evil eye. Alice ran over to her friend and put her arm around her. The girl was crying. Alice had never seen her friend cry; Sharkie had always said that only weak people cried.

Sharkie seemed to melt into a much smaller person, and Alice gave her friend an extra hug.

'Glad it's you,' said Miranda thickly under a coating of tears. 'If anyone, deserved to win, apart from me, it is you.'

Alice locked this generous praise away and turned to face Miranda. 'You were the fastest one, you know, it was just luck I won.'

'Sometimes you deserve to have some luck,' replied Sharkie, sounding remarkably mature. She then gave her runny nose a tremendous blow with a holey tissue, wiped her red eyes and tried to smile.

'Come on, I'm starving. Let's see what your mum and my mum brought for our sports day picnic. The hamper weighed a tonne, I had to carry it all the way here, as Jodie and Clara were being naturally unhelpful. I hope they brought ice cream in a cool box. I feel like I need four choc ices to cool me down.'

XxxxxxxxxxxX

The Picnic

There was plenty of ice cream.

As much as Ella would have liked to congratulate her sister on the finish line, she had to duly wait till the Orchestra of Sports was dismissed for lunch. When she arrived, Hazel was sitting cross-legged on the cashmere rug, happily playing with a small glow-in-the-dark skeleton. Dr Brunel had kindly given her the little model and she was intently learning all the bones in the human body. There were over two hundred, so she was in quiet concentration, determined to learn them all off by heart.

Alice was lying spread-eagled on the grass, spraying water from her sports bottle on herself in attempt to cool her hot limbs after all the exercise. She clutched the gold running medal in her sweaty palms, scared that if she let go, the whole event would disappear into a forgotten dream.

Miranda was still looking a little red-eyed after her unfortunate running race experience with the Winston's College girl. However, Ella and Jodie were making her feel better by profusely apologising that a girl at their school could be so badly behaved.

'We are never talking to Violet again!' said Ella. 'We have told all our friends not to speak to her either! Jodie nodded in keen agreement, 'Yep, I have deleted her phone number from as many of my friends' mobile phones contacts as possible.' (Indeed, this was a slight understatement as Jodie had seized all the phones of Year Seven that she could, sometimes having to convince her fellow Winston College classmates to delete the phone number by force. Jodie, though not as sporty as her sister Miranda, was still quite strong and perfectly persuasive when required.) She then resumed comforting her twin. 'Clara's mum has even un-invited *her* mum from all of her future parent networking social evenings.'

Hazel chimed in, warning that the girl's action could have caused both of them to fracture several of their bones. She then began to list all the bones in the leg, but the rest of the picnic party seemed curiously uninterested.

Mum and Bella smiled at each other. After many years of argument together, Triple Trouble and the Terrible Two had finally learnt to appreciate their differences. Perhaps they were beginning to grow up. Now that was a scary thought.

9. Count Down

'Hv u been rvisng all nite?'

'Mayb.'

'U'll b gr8.'

'No, it's 2 late!'

Ella crossed her fingers.

She was already on holiday; her school was the first to break up for the summer. However, Alice and Hazel had one final week before they were free and for them it was exam week. Despite her sisters telling her how lucky she was, Ella didn't actually feel that lucky to already be free from school.

Ella would never admit it but it was a bit boring, not having their company during the day. She spent most of the time with Astrid. They had decided to start a music band and had roped in Clara and Jodie too. This was mainly out of kindness because neither of them was that talented at their instruments. However, they thought a band needed at least four members to exist. They called themselves "Musica!"—the Latin word for music. Needless to say, Ella had chosen the band name.

Hazel emerged from her duvet hugging her geography, history and science text books. Ayushi had determinedly told anyone who'd listen that if you slept on your text books, you did seven per cent (on average) better in your exams. Hazel had not tested the theory; instead, she had been reading her books all night with the light of her phone. Now she had a headache. She regretted her midnight revision. She must have fallen asleep in the last hour of the early morning and it felt like all the knowledge had seeped out of her head in weird dreams.

Alice leapt out of bed and as was customary now, began to stretch as if she was preparing for a sports race then and there. She was looking fresh and unperturbed. Her "behaviour and progress" reports were still emailed on a weekly basis to Mum and Dad. They already knew that she was doing okay, so the idea of exams was considerably less scary than a sports competition. She just was counting down to the holidays.

XxxxxxxxxxxX

Hazel

Alphabetical order was tiresome.

Hazel stood in the playground in the blazing sunshine. She was hopping up and down nervously in her row "P". She had miserably waved goodbye to

Ayushi, who had left her to go to the "S" line and Patrick, who had gone far away to the "B" line.

The main assembly hall was all set up for the dreaded end of term examinations. Hazel felt butterflies flap in her stomach violently. Alice had joked at breakfast that this must be her favourite week of the year, a chance to show off her "brainy box". Ella had been more sympathetic but had reasoned rather too logically for Hazel's liking, that as she had done nothing but revise all year, she would be great. Oh, if only they understood, thought Hazel and she jogged up and down in line "P" to rid herself of nervous energy.

Ayushi was the best at understanding her fears. 'This is a milestone in our academic lives,' she said seriously over flapjacks at break. (Patrick was convinced the flapjack oats gave them extra brain power.) 'It's make or break!'

The bell rang and Dr Grey gave them the thumbs up. 'Good luck, my mini professors!' he called encouragingly. 'Just remember your CSI school triumph last term.'

Hazel attempted to grin back as she remembered their chromatography crime solving success at the university last term. She followed the back of line "O" and sat down at the small wooden desk marked "H Platt". One day she thought it would say "Dr H Platt". The papers were given out by the headmistress and Hazel took a deep breath. To her delight, she noticed that the exam was printed on pale purple paper. Well that was a lucky sign.

'On your marks, get set, go!' called the headmistress as if she was starting a sports race. There was a great rustling as a hundred exam papers were opened and feet shuffled to get comfortable under the old-fashioned wooden desks.

Hazel flicked onto the first paper and smiled. The first question was all about chromatography.

Time to begin her journey to becoming a science professor.

XxxxxxxxxxxX

That Night

Glass broke for a reason.

Ella listened. Scared. Wide awake. Found her phone and speedily texted her sisters.

'Did u hear tht?'

'Arghhh. What?'

'Listen!'

There was a dull thud coming from the downstairs sitting room. Even Hazel had stuck her nose from under the warm bed clothes and listened intently.

Alice looked at her sisters and put her fingers on her lips to indicate complete silence. She leapt out of bed with the agility of a cat and crept to the door. There was an unmistakable sound of something/someone bumping into furniture downstairs.

'It's a burglar!' whispered Ella, trembling. 'We are all going to die!'

Hazel snorted at the normally calm Ella. 'Don't be silly, Ella. Burglars steal stuff, they wouldn't want to disturb us, we would get in their way.'

Alice grabbed an old tennis racket from an open wardrobe and rallied her troops. 'Come on. Let's sort this out.'

Hazel thought it a good idea to arm themselves with some sort of weapon, so she grabbed a particularly heavy science encyclopaedia, which she could drop on a poor unsuspecting burglar's head. Ella followed her example and opened her violin case to take out her bow. She carried it as a knight would carry a sword and slowly followed her sisters down the stairs.

The noise was getting louder as they reached the sitting room. The door was closed and Alice reached for the handle. At that point, the tension was too much for Ella and she uttered a loud scream.

'Mum! Dad! There's a murderer in the sitting room!' shouted an unnerved Ella and she then pelted up the stairs.

Alice rolled her eyes, 'Ella would make a rubbish spy. She has totally blown our cover now.'

There was an excited motion from the sitting room and then silence fell.

'What on earth is all that racket?' Dad asked. He appeared at the top of the stairs, still half asleep and wearing his dressing gown inside out.

Mum appeared with Ella trying to hide behind her and stopped to witness the peculiar sight of her children, armed with a tennis racket and violin bow, crouching by the sitting room door.

Dad, rushed downstairs and beckoned the kids to go up the stairs to safety. He threw Mum the phone, uttering, 'If anything happens, Katie, darling call the police.'

'Oh, Robin,' exclaimed Mum worriedly, 'Take care, darling.'

Dad put his hand on the door handle, took a deep breath and flung it open. He switched on the light. The room in its illuminated state looked decidedly un-scary, Alice decided.

The room, although very messy, had no burglar present. In fact, as Hazel surveyed the crime scene she decided it was odd because nothing was missing. The window was wide open and Dad's newspaper was scrunched up on the floor over a pile of Hazel's puzzle books. The cushions were decorating the room all over the place and Ella's music stand looked like the Leaning Tower of Pisa as it was bent on one side as if something heavy had sat on it. There was a puddle of water on the coffee table and the poor tulips, which had been happily placed in a glass vase, were now strewn over the sofa.

'Hello?' said Mum, who was now speaking into the phone receiver. 'Is that the police? I think we have had a break-in.'

XxxxxxxxxxxX

Ella

It was impossible to sleep.

Ella lay in bed wide awake. She was plagued by irrational thoughts. What if the burglar was still here in the house? He could have hidden in the coat cupboard. The person clearly didn't like Ella, as they had destroyed her music stand. She shivered at the thought. She bravely sat up and looked across at Alice; she was snoring loudly. Alice slept deeply due to the intense daily sport schedule. Ella then saw Hazel, who was hugging her favourite science magazine, *Chemical Cartoons*, and snoring like a mouse in comparison to Alice.

Ella had done brilliantly in her end of term exams, yet she still seemed to be sleeping off the exhaustion. Mum and Dad were glad that at least she could have some free time in the holidays to recover. Her school report came through a week into the holidays. Mum had opened the letter and gaped. She had handed it over to Dad, who half choked on his morning cup of coffee.

For the next week, nothing changed. Ella insisted that she slept with her violin case open, so that if an intruder entered the bedroom she could easily seize her bow to defend herself. Alice and Hazel, glad it was finally holidays, slept fine, but Ella looked more tired by the day as she couldn't believe that they were safe in their house any more.

Each morning, Mum and Dad had a phone conversation with a policeman about the break-in.

'Any updates?' the triplets would always ask, but the answer was always 'no'.

Exactly a week later, however, a policeman visited their house. Dad answered the door and was surprised to see that he was looking rather happy.

'Good news, Mr Platt. Good news! We have finally found our burglar!'

XxxxxxxxxxxxX

One Week Later

'Girls, you have a visitor.'

Dad smiled as the three triplets cautiously approached the sitting room. After the break-in, it had been restored to its usual state of tidiness. Mum had felt bad that Ella's music stand had been ruined by the intruder and had bought her a special replacement in pink. In front of this new sparkling pink music stand was a tartan quilted basket. In the basket, there was a small green teddy bear and lying curled up wagging his tail next to the teddy bear was —

'Baby Bear!' exclaimed Alice.

'How did he find us?' asked Ella, not daring to believe her luck. 'Can we keep him?'

Dad and Mum nodded in agreement.

'We must call Baby Bear a proper name, like Perkins!' pleaded an excited Hazel, eager to have their new pet named after an eminent scientist. 'And get him a purple collar!'

'No, no, Baby Bear is cooler than that, we should call him Bolt,' said Alice, inspired by a well-known runner.

'What about Canis?' asked Ella hesitantly, instantly thinking that Baby Bear should be called after the Latin word for dog. 'Then we could have a sign on our house which said, *Cave canem*, which means, "beware of the dog".'

Dad and Mum laughed at the certainly different name suggestions. Dad sighed relief. Fair enough, they may have been arguing about the name of the dog but at least they now owned something that they universally liked. After all their differences this year, they finally had something which brought them together again. Mum and Dad had thought long and hard about how to encourage the triplets to spend more time with one another now they were in separate schools. Then their burglar had provided the solution.

'Say hello to your burglar, Ella!' chuckled Dad.

Ella stopped hugging Baby Bear for a moment and turned around, looking confused. 'What do you mean, Dad?'

'Well, Baby Bear was the burglar. He escaped from the vet's and don't ask me how, but he managed to find our house. You must have left quite an impression on him when you met him on the train travelling back from Birmingham and he somehow tracked down our scent. Once he found our house he entered through an open window in our sitting room. Now, I shall not enquire which of you three, Triple Trouble, forgot to close the window, but anyway, Baby Bear saw an opportunity open!'

Hazel digested this information quietly and then asked the logical question. 'But if he was at the vet's, surely his owners will want him back when he is better?'

'The owners moved house and they weren't allowed a pet in their new place. So, they gave him to the vet to find a home for him again. However, it seems as if Baby Bear took matters into his own hands.'

Right on cue, Baby Bear, looking even more adorable than when they had last seen him a few months ago, thumped his tail on the floor and put his paws over his eyes.

'Oh!' sighed a relieved Ella. 'Dog is honestly the cutest burglar in the world. How could I have been scared of him?' Ella then resumed to hug the little dog as if to apologise for her previous mistrust of his kindliness.

'Why don't you pick his name out of a hat?' said Dad.

Out of thin air, Alice produced her yellow school swim hat. 'Okay, write the names and put them in here, then Mum can pick out the winning name.'

The triplets hastily scribbled the names and put them in the hat. 'Okay, girls, close your eyes. Baby bear is to be called—Bolt!''

'Hurrah!' Alice punched the air victoriously with her fist. The other two grimaced in defeat. However, they secretly thought that Bolt was quite a cool name for a dog.

Alice then turned to her sisters. 'But Bolt will need a middle name and surname, so his full name is Bolt Canis Perkins.'

Ella went over to Bolt and ceremoniously shook his paw. 'Welcome to the family, Bolt Canis Perkins! I shall be your classics and music teacher.'

Hazel approved of the formalities and copied her sister in shaking Bolt's paw. (Luckily, he was a patient dog.) 'Welcome to the family, Bolt Canis Perkins, you are partly named after an important scientist. Lucky you. I shall be your science and maths teacher.'

Finally, Alice bounded over to the dog and took his well shaken paw. 'Welcome, Bolt!' she said, looking at him seriously. 'I am Alice and I will be responsible for your daily fitness routine. I will draw you up a timetable of your daily walks with me. I am good at sport, so I am sure you will be too!'

Bolt bowed his head to each of the three sisters in turn and then as if to answer them, barked a big friendly-sounding, 'Woof' in agreement.

That night, all three sisters, including Ella, slept well. As it was Bolt's first night, as a special treat he was allowed to sleep in the triplets' bedroom. Ella had already been busy and cross-stitched a little sign, which said "Cave Canem" (Latin for 'Beware of the Dog') – in pink thread, of course – and laid it across his basket as a door/paw mat. Above the tartan basket, Alice had stuck a busy-looking time table of the daily walking times of Bolt. Finally, Hazel had bought a purple collar for Bolt and put a little periodic table in his basket for some bedtime reading.

Dad and Mum looked in at the three sleeping sisters. Home for the holidays, together at last, united by a most unexpected new family member.

THE END